THE DALTON BRIDES:
The Cowboy's
Mail-Order Bride

KIT
MORGAN
BESTSELLING
AUTHOR

ANGEL CREEK PRESS
The Dalton Brides:
The Cowboy's Mail-Order Bride
(A Dalton Mail-Order Bride Romance)
by Kit Morgan

DEDICATION

To the wonderful ladies and gentlemen of Pioneer Hearts. And because you asked ...

NOTE

This prologue is available as a separate e-book titled *The Escape*, as well as in both other books in this series, *The Rancher's Mail-Order Bride* and *The Drifter's Mail-Order Bride*.

To find out about my upcoming releases and to keep up to date on all the crazy happenings in Clear Creek, the wackiest town in the old west, sign up for The Clear Creek Gazette at http://www.authorkitmorgan.com/

PROLOGUE

The Brothers

Walton Dalton stood in the middle of his land, knowing he'd found his place in the world. The two sections next to his were both open, and he was staking claim for his brothers. The three of them would own a huge section of Texas dirt, and they would ranch it together.

Walton was the oldest of three brothers. They didn't like to be reminded that he was the oldest though. With only fifteen minutes difference between him and his brother, Nate, and twenty-five minutes between him and Bart, they preferred to all think of themselves as the same age. They weren't though. Walton was always aware of his burden as the eldest. He had to be the strongest, fastest and best of the three, so that he could live up to what was expected of him.

He hadn't built his house yet, so he sat down right there in the dirt to write letters to his brothers, asking them to join him. He knew they would. He'd always been the ringleader of the three of them, and even as adults, he was certain he could convince them ranching was the way for them to gain wealth and happiness.

Rather than writing two different letters, he just wrote one and copied it for the other. When he was finished, he had two letters that read the same.

My Dear Brother,

I'm writing you from a section of land that I'm about to begin homesteading in north Texas. The two sections beside me are available. I'd like for the three of us to claim this land and build a ranching empire here in the Lone Star State. We could have land for as far as the eye can see, and the prairie here is so flat you can see a long way.

I'm about a half day's ride south of a town called Weatherford, which is west of Fort Worth. If you get to the area, people will know me. No one forgets a Dalton.

I hope you'll consider joining me here, because I need you both. There's enough work for twenty men, but between the three of us, I know we can do the work of thirty. Remember what Pa always said? "When you three team up, nothing can stop you." The local ranchers won't know what hit them once the Dalton brothers make their mark.

I'm going to start building my cabin. When you two get here, we'll build a couple more houses and get us some ladies. It's time.

Don't take too long to get here. Land is going fast.

Sincerely,
Walt

He folded both of the letters and got to his feet. His spirited stallion danced away from him, as if he was trying to get him to not settle down. "We're here to stay, Spirit. No more wandering for us."

Walton and Spirit had done more than their share of traveling. He had spent the last ten years as a cowboy, learning the ins and outs of ranching. He was finally ready to start a life, and he was going to do it.

He swung up onto Spirit and rode him into town. It was an hour to the closest small town of Wiggieville, but he knew that with his two brothers' help, they would soon have a bustling town right there. He could picture it already.

For the life of him, Bart Dalton couldn't figure out how his brother Walt had tracked him down. He'd only ridden into the bustling city of San Francisco the day before, after all, and hadn't even planned on stopping there. How in high heaven did Walt know to send a letter to the San Francisco post office before Bart even knew he was going there?

Bart had been on his way from running an apple-picking crew in the Yakima River Valley in the Washington Territory to a new California village called Hollywood when he hooked up with a couple of other drifters like himself. They said they were headed for Frisco, so he tagged along. It wasn't like he had any pressing business in Hollywood, he just thought the name sounded nice. He could almost see massive groves of holly trees surrounding the little community.

As he thought back on his last letter to his brothers — he always wrote one and just copied it for the other — he recalled saying something about California. But that was months ago. As far as Walt and Nate knew, he could have come and gone by then.

But it had always been like that with them. No matter how much distance separated them, they always seemed to know in their gut what was happening with the others. Like that time Walt got bucked from a horse he was trying to break and got a concussion.

Bart had been dealing faro in a Kansas City gambling hell at the time, and an overwhelming urge to sleep came over him. Somehow he knew Walt had been injured so he walked right out of that hell, jumped on his trusty horse Roamer, and rode east in the direction of St. Louis.

By the time he arrived several days later, Walt was up and around, and didn't seem the least bit surprised Bart had shown up. Nate arrived a few hours later. They all had a good laugh, and spent a few days reminiscing and catching up before Bart's feet started itching to get back on the road. That was the last time he'd seen his brothers, and he missed them something fierce.

Being triplets, they'd always been close but, aside from his brothers, no one ever let Bart forget he was the youngest, even though it was only by minutes. Walt was the bossy older brother and Nate was the no-nonsense one. Everyone expected Bart to be the wild one of the bunch, the irresponsible younger brother, and he was all too happy to oblige.

He'd get into all sorts of trouble and blame it on his brothers. Of course, they did the same to him, so it evened out in the end. He pretended it was all in good fun, but deep down he felt empty, like something was missing. It was like he hadn't yet found his true identity, and everyone's expectations — or lack of them — were holding him back from discovering it.

As he and his brothers grew older, he felt stifled at his family home in Oregon City. His brothers seemed perfectly content helping out around the dairy farm, but Bart knew there was so much more out in the world than milking cows and shoveling manure. He wanted to see it all. Maybe once he saw everything there was to see, he'd settle down and live a 'normal' life, but until that day, he'd never be truly happy.

The day after their seventeenth birthday, Bart woke up ready to break the news to his brothers: He was leaving and didn't know when or if he'd ever see them again. He was giddy with excitement but also heartbroken at the idea of leaving them.

They were a part of him and he was having trouble imagining life without them, but he had to do this. As much as he wanted them to come with him, he had to strike out on his own and find that elusive thing that was missing from his soul.

His gut churned as he crept through the quiet house in the early morning hours. He'd get Roamer saddled and packed, then go wake his brothers. If he was lucky, he'd be able to sneak away without waking his folks. Ma would have a fit and Pa might refuse to let him go. He longed to say goodbye but it would be too risky.

Stepping into the barn, he was stopped in his tracks by the sight of his entire family — Ma, Pa, Walt and Nate — standing around an already-saddled and fully loaded Roamer. Tears were streaming down Ma's plump cheeks, and Pa had a comforting arm wrapped around her shoulders. Walt had a worried look on his face and Nate just looked irritated. Only Pa was smiling, even though it held a twinge of sadness.

"How did you know?" Bart stammered in surprise.

Pa tilted his head at Walt and Nate. "Your brothers told us. You didn't tell them?" He chuckled and shook his head. "Figgers."

"I packed you several days worth of food," sniffled his mother. "Don't eat it all at once. I can't stand the thought of you starving out on the trail."

"Yes, Ma," he whispered, humbled at his family's support and love. Why hadn't he trusted that they would understand?

Walt sidled up to him and slapped him on the back. "You'll be fine out there, Bart, but you know if you ever need anything, me and Nate are here for ya."

"I know, brother."

As irritated as Nate looked, he still pulled Bart into a fierce hug. "Don't be stupid."

Bart smiled. It was an old joke between them, going back to when they were little kids. He returned his brother's hug, and soon his whole family had their arms wrapped around him.

Pa was the first to pull away. Clearing his throat of emotion, he croaked, "Sun's fixing to come up, son. Best you get while the getting's good."

Bart gritted his teeth as he rode out of the barn, willing himself to not look back. If he looked back, he might change his mind, and the last thing he wanted was to be stuck in Oregon City for the rest of his life.

Leaving his family behind was the hardest thing he'd ever had to do. And in the ten years he'd spent rambling around the country, it remained at the top of the list.

Rereading Walt's letter, Bart bristled a bit at the commanding tone. Walt always assumed the others would do whatever he told them to, like he was their ringleader or something simply by virtue of being a few minutes older. Bart had spent much of his youth rebelling against his oldest brother's overbearing ways, and he was amused to find the instinct was still there. Some things never changed.

"Whatcha got there, Bart?"

Bart was startled out of his reverie by one of his latest riding companions. Chuck was his name, and he was as shifty a drifter as Bart had ever met. And he'd met a lot. He would never dream of doing business with the man, but Chuck was pleasant enough to pass the time with on the trail.

"Oh, just a letter from my brother, inviting me to settle near him in Texas," Bart replied, carefully folding the letter and slipping it into an inner pocket he'd had sewn into his duster.

"Oh, yeah?" Chuck's eyes sparkled as he leaned back against the wall of the post office next to Bart.

"I hear they're giving away land left and right out there. Whereabouts is he settling?"

There was an unspoken code among drifters like them: Never ask personal questions. Too many men were running from something, and all were suspicious by nature, so it was best to keep your questions to yourself.

Obviously Chuck hadn't learned that lesson yet.

"North, I think," Bart evaded.

Chuck took the hint and nodded sagely, as if that explained everything. "You goin'?"

The man's question took him by surprise. He honestly hadn't even thought about it. He'd been too wrapped up in memories.

"I dunno." And he really didn't. He'd been moving around so much over the years that he didn't think he'd know how to sit still for very long, even if he was so inclined.

Which he wasn't.

But something tugged at his insides, remembering the day he rode away from his family. He'd do anything for them, and now Walt was asking for his help. *I hope you'll consider joining me here, because I need you both.* That was as close to begging as Walt ever got.

Bart was honestly surprised that his brothers hadn't married and settled down by now. They'd both always been more traditional and down-to-earth than he had ever dreamed of being — or ever wanted to be.

But at 27, they were a bit overdue in starting their own families. He ached for them a little because they'd both always talked about having a bunch of young'uns running around. He didn't really understand it but he felt bad for them that they didn't have it yet.

Resolve settled in his belly like a glowing coal. His brothers would do anything for him, and had already helped him out of more jams than he cared to think about. Walt was right; it was time. Time to return the favor.

He'd ride out to Texas and help Walt and Nate set up their ranch, even if it took a year or two. It was the least he could do. When everything was rolling along, and his brothers had a couple of nice wives — maybe even some babies — he'd leave his portion to them and continue his search for whatever was missing in his life.

"'Scuse me," he mumbled to Chuck and strode back into the post office.

Walt,
You can count on me, brother.
Bart

"Get him, Nate!"

A growing crowd of townspeople and cowhands cheered as Nate Dalton landed face first in the dirt. He rolled to his back and, with lightning speed — at least it felt like it, considering the blow he'd been dealt — climbed to his feet to face his opponent. The dirty chuck-eater clobbered him with a piece of firewood, and even now held it before him like a shield.

"Seems we have a difference of opinion," Nate told him as he wiped away the blood trickling down one side of his face. This had to be the worst cattle drive he'd ever been on.

The Easterner, a man Nate figured had no business changing the price per head, swallowed hard and raised the wood as if to hit him again. The difference was, this time he faced Nate instead of sneaking up on him like he did when he'd struck him the first time.

"As Mr. Meyer's du...duly... appointed representative..." he stammered, "I must ask you to concede to the new price given."

Nate shook his head against a bout of dizziness, and hoped he didn't have a concussion like the one his brother Walt did a few years back. For a scant second he wondered if his two brothers would show up to check on him as they'd done for Walt.

The thought was lost however when the good-for-nothing dandy took another swing at him. Nate ducked and dodged, and blocked the next blow with one fist as he punched the low-life in the face with the other to send him sprawling. "I'll do my business with Mr. Meyers, if you don't mind."

The man didn't get up. In fact, he didn't respond at all. Nate stared at him a moment as Sam Wheeler, one of his drovers, slapped him on the back. "You showed him!"

Nate leaned forward and peered at the unconscious form. At least he hoped he was unconscious. He didn't hit him that hard, did he? "Where's Meyers? How come he sent this idiot for me to deal with?"

"He's at his ranch. I hear tell from folks down at the post office his wife is having a baby. That's why this yellow-belly is in town."

"This yellow-belly tried to gouge the price per head. Now I'll have to ride out to the Meyers' ranch to get our business done."

Sam looked at the man on the ground. A couple of their fellow cowboys tried to get him to come around by slapping the side of his face a few times. "Maybe you should take this fool back with ya and tell Mr. Meyers what he did?"

"Won't have to," Nate said. "This is a small town, with enough people here to let Meyers know what happened. I'll wager this duffer to be out of a job come suppertime."

"Oh, good point," said Sam as he reached into his pocket. "I almost forgot, here's a letter for ya."

"A letter?"

"Yeah, it's from your brother. He wants ya to come to Texas."

Nate's eyes narrowed. "You read my mail?"

"No help for it! There's a tear in the envelope, see?" he said and pointed. "Is it my fault if'n the letter fell out?"

Nate rolled his eyes and shook his head in exasperation. It hurt. He winced as he touched his wound and blinked a few times to clear his vision. He was tired of dealing with ranchers who didn't know how to run their business or make a good profit. He hoped whatever Walt wrote didn't add to an already disastrous cattle drive. He unfolded the letter and studied it, but the words were too blurry for him to read. Not a good sign.

"Looks like the dandy got ya a good one," said the grizzled cowhand as he stared at Nate's head. "Want me to read your letter for ya?"

"I'll be fine, go make sure that idiot is still alive, will ya? And then tell the rest of the boys to wait for me. I'll be back."

"Where ya goin'?"

"Post office." He strode past Sam and headed down the street. He didn't get far when another bout of dizziness hit, and he slowed his pace to keep from falling over. He'd been hit in the head before, be it from a fist, a kick, or the occasional hard object, but this particular hit, coupled with Walt's letter, managed to do something Nate hadn't yet. It knocked some sense into him. "Sense" being the operative word.

Nate used to have his share of good sense at one time, the type other men respected and sought out so they could benefit too. Nate, being as sensible as he was, gave his advice freely. Not only did he give it, he was willing to receive it.

Except for a piece of advice given him by his last employer, one Thomas Adams, who advised Nate to stay away from his daughters, or else. The "or else" meant Nate would decorate a cottonwood come morning if Mr. Adams found any of his precious daughters compromised.

Nate wasn't stupid and, lucky for him, wasn't attracted to any of the four women. This made it easy to stay away from them. Keeping them away from him, on the other hand, was another matter.

Two of them snuck into the bunkhouse one night. A third rode out to where he and some of the men were branding cattle. If he'd listened to his good sense, he'd have high-tailed it off the Adams' spread pronto. But no... Instead, Lucretia, the fourth and most aggressive of the bunch, launched herself at him the same night in the foyer of the ranch house. She flung her arms around his neck and kissed him as her father came down the stairs.

Nate barely escaped with his life.

But his ordeal with the Adams sisters was behind him, and he wanted to keep it that way. If there was one thing he couldn't stand, it was a forward female trying to rope him into matrimony. He would marry when he was good and ready, not to mention settle down.

Nate reached the post office and leaned against the door a moment before going in. By now his head throbbed something awful. He unfolded Walton's letter and took another stab at reading it. It wasn't easy, but he managed. After several moments he refolded the missive and stuck it back into a shirt pocket.

"Texas," he muttered to himself. "Looks like you found yourself a sweet deal, big brother." But was he ready to join him?

"Good Lord!" A woman cried to his left. "What happened to you?"

Nate stared at her, a bemused look on his face. She pointed to his head and gasped. "Oh, yeah. Sorry ma'am. I...got cut ...shaving."

The woman shook her head and made a tsk, tsk, tsk, sound. "You'd best get that taken care of. What were you doing? Trying to shave your head with an ax?"

"A piece of wood, actually," Nate said drily. "Bad barber." He turned and headed for the postmaster.

"Yes?" said a wiry little man behind the counter. He peered at Nate over his spectacles and gasped louder than the woman. "Egad! You're bleeding!"

"I've been informed. Do you have any other mail for me? The name's Nate Dalton." It would be like Sam to bring only the one letter and leave everything else. The postmaster grimaced one more time before he turned to search for any remaining mail.

Nate and the other drovers only came to Fountain, Colorado once every couple of months. As it was more frequent than other places he'd been cow punching, it was as good a place as any to have his mail sent.

"No sir, Mr. Dalton," the postmaster announced as he turned around. "Nothing else here. Lucky you came into town when you did, that letter arrived only a week ago."

"Much obliged," said Nate as he turned and headed for the door. As he stepped onto the boardwalk a thought struck. After he sold his employer's stock, collected the money, and headed back, he wouldn't have another chance to answer Walton's letter until the next time they brought in more cattle.

He stared at the dirt in the street in indecision. He could still taste the same dirt in his mouth. He let out a weary sigh, took his brother's letter out of his pocket, and stared at it a moment.

"Texas ..." he mused. Walt wanted to settle down, start an empire, not to mention a family. Was he ready to do that?

A man crossing the street caught Nate's eye. The man was heading toward the post office. Nate reached out and stopped him before he could go inside. "Hey mister, where's the doctor in this town?"

"Go down to the end of the street, turn left, and you'll find him. I think he just got back from the Meyers' ranch." He looked at Nate and let out a low whistle. "I think you'd best hurry and have him tend ya." The man shuddered, pulled out of Nate's hold, and went into the post office.

Nate watched him go, before he looked in the direction he'd indicated. As he started off, he wondered if Bart answered their brother yet. Would he be ready to settle down? Of the three, Bart had the worst case of itchy feet.

Nate could wander as well as the next, but he at least stuck in one place for a while before moving on. Sometimes he'd stay in one spot a couple of years. Bart was lucky to stay in one place a couple of months. But in his gut, Nate knew Bart had answered their brother's call.

He reached the doctor's house, stuffed Walt's letter into his pocket again, and went inside.

"Jumpin' Jehoshaphat!" An elderly man cried when he saw him. "What happened to you?"

"Never mind, are you the doctor?" asked Nate. "I need me a piece of paper and something to write with. I got a letter here needs answering."

"Letter? I'd say let it wait, son. That gash on your forehead needs tendin'. Let me get a few things and I'll fix ya right up."

"My letter needs tending more than I do."

"What's so important it can't wait until after I fix your wound?"

Nate gave him a broad smile. "Cause I gotta let my big brother know I'm gonna settle in Texas!"

The doctor gawked at him, shook his head, and went to fetch him paper, pen, and ink.

Dear Walt,
Count me in.
Nate

Walton worked hard to build a small house while he waited for his brothers' replies. Twice a week he would ride into town for fresh supplies and see if there were any new letters.

Finally, more than a month after he'd mailed his letters there was one from Bart. Walton read it right there in the store and smiled. One of his brothers would be there any day, and they'd start building their empire. The Daltons were going make their mark on Texas.

It took another week before he received a later from Nate. He was coming, too. All of the brothers would soon be together.

By the middle of August, they had constructed three small cabins in the middle of the property, and they had a growing herd of cattle. Walton had noticed an advertisement in the local paper for mail order brides. He knew Bart had no intention of marrying, and Nate wanted to wait until the ranch was more stable, but they were younger than him, after all. By the time their brides arrived, they'd understand his need to have a family.

After their supper of beans and beans that evening, Walton's brothers went home and left him alone as they did every night. He sat at his small table and wrote a letter.

Dear Miss Miller,

My brothers and I have a large ranch about an hour out of Wiggieville, Texas. We've built three houses here and have the start of a good herd of cattle. That means we're ready to marry. We're identical triplets, so we're all about six foot with brown hair and brown eyes. We're strong men and perfectly capable of providing for brides and any little ones that may come along.

We're twenty-seven, and would really like women between the ages of eighteen and twenty-six. Looks aren't terribly important, but they need to be willing to work hard and cook well. We're all sick of eating our own cooking.

I look forward to your response.

Sincerely,

Walton, Nate and Bart Dalton

Walton folded the letter and set it aside. He'd mail it when he went to town for supplies the next morning. Soon, they'd have women doing their cooking and cleaning. Not to mention keeping them warm at night. Walton smiled. He liked the idea of a little lady to keep him warm at night more than he was willing to express.

The Sisters

Gwen Blue hurried through the dark streets of Beckham. Why had Gertie wanted to meet her so late at night? She was going to be married to Stanley in just a couple of weeks, so she wasn't certain why the woman would want to meet her most bitter enemy at all, but she'd go. The letter had said something about mending fences, which sounded good to Gwen after a lifetime of hateful rivalry.

When she arrived at the schoolhouse where they had once been classmates, she looked around. She'd always loved this playground, but it seemed different at night. It was scary.

Stanley stepped around the schoolhouse and walked to her. "Oh, Gwen, I'm so glad you've come!"

Gwen looked at her old suitor with surprise. "What are you doing here?" Stanley stepped closer to her, and Gwen took a step back. "I was supposed to be meeting Gertie."

Stanley reached out and touched her cheek. "I wrote that letter, Gwen. I can't marry Gertie when I'm still in love with you. I never should have broken off our courtship. Will you forgive me and give me another chance?"

Gwen stared at him in disbelief before finally shaking her head. "First, let's get one thing straight. You did not break off our courtship. I did. I broke it off when I saw you looking at Gertie's bosom after church one day. Second, you brought me here under false pretenses? No, I will not forgive you. No, I will not take you back. You need to marry Gertie like you promised. If you don't, everyone will always know what a cad you are. Don't contact me again."

Gwen was practically shaking with anger as she spun on her heel to go back home. She'd thought she and Gertie would be able to put their past behind them. No, it was just Stanley being selfish once again.

Stanley put his hand on Gwen's shoulder and spun her back around. "You know you still love me!"

He crushed his lips to hers, and she stomped on his foot to get him to release her. How had she ever thought she loved this man? "Let go of me, you fool!" She tore away from him and rushed away. She never should have come.

Two days later at church, Gwen sat with her sisters, Bonnie and Libby, wondering why the ladies of the church refused to speak to her on her way to the pew. Some even moved their dresses out of the way to keep them from touching her. She felt like a pariah, and she didn't even know what she'd done to be treated that way.

Bonnie and Libby had received the same treatment for the most part, but no one had avoided getting touched by them. Gwen had always been the most popular girl in their entire congregation, with men flocking around her, but that had changed as well. Even her current sweetheart, Norbert Rumfield, had refused to speak to her. She didn't know what people thought she'd done, but she certainly hadn't. Whatever it was.

Their mother took her seat on the other side of Bonnie, and leaned over glaring at Gwen. "Why do all my friends think you're pregnant?"

Gwen stared back at her mother, her mind spinning. Pregnant? Yes, she'd probably kissed a few more boys than she should have over the years, but she'd never even let one of them touch her breast. No, she wasn't pregnant. Who would say that?

"I have no idea, Mama. I'm not. I swear!"

Bonnie and Libby snickered. They loved it when Gwen was in trouble. She always shamed them because she was always kissing all the boys. There weren't enough men in town when Gwen was around.

Sarah Blue looked back and forth between her oldest and youngest daughters. "What are you two laughing about? Rumors also say the two of you were seen kissing the same boy! Where did I go wrong?"

Bonnie and Libby exchanged glances. "Never!" Bonnie exclaimed. "I've never even kissed one man, Mama."

Libby shook her head. "Gwen always beats us to the boys. We never get a chance to kiss them."

Gwen glared at Libby. "I can't believe you just said that! I hate you!" She stood up and ran out of the church. People were saying mean horrible things about her, and she wasn't about to put up with it.

When she got outside, she wiped away her tears. Leaning against the back of the church, she sighed. Why were people always willing to believe bad things about her? No, she wasn't an angel and never pretended to be. But she wasn't a whore, and that's what people were making her out to be, and it just wasn't fair.

She did just as much volunteer work as the next woman and worked hard to make certain she always looked her best. It wasn't like she was shallow, she just felt like the orphans in town deserved to see a pretty woman and not one with her hair all down around her shoulders looking scraggly.

She sat there for a minute before she realized her nemesis from her schooldays, Gertie Landry, was glaring at her. "I heard you kissed my beau in the park late one night this week," she sneered. "He's still marrying me, though."

Gwen looked at Gertie. Had she started the rumors? "I didn't kiss him. He forced a kiss on me. I told him I'm not interested in renewing our relationship. That's what he wants, you know. He wants me to take him back so he won't have to marry you."

Gwen knew her words were mean, but there were times when she just couldn't hold back, and just looking at Gertie had made her angry for years. Ever since the other girl had pushed her in the mud when she was on her way to her first church social.

She hadn't been able to clean up enough, and Gertie had danced with her beau. Spiteful girl.

Gertie walked closer. "That's not true! He told me what happened. You saw him and ran to him in the park, demanding he break off our engagement, and then you flung your arms around his neck and kissed him. You're a tramp, Gwen Blue!"

"Did you start the rumors about me being pregnant?" Gwen stood up and faced the other girl.

"Now you won't be able to entice all the men you meet." Gertie smirked at Gwen.

"People are going to know you lied."

"By then I'll be happily married. Besides, I'll tell them you lost the baby. No big deal."

Gwen felt a growl rising in her throat. Never in her life had she wanted to hit anyone as much as she wanted to hit Gertie at that moment. She knew it was the wrong thing to do, but she just couldn't help herself. She balled up her fist, just like her brothers had taught her, and she punched Gertie right in the eye.

Gertie let out a loud wail, her hand covering her eye. Gwen stood there, knowing people would come to see what the ruckus was about. She planned to tell everyone right there and then that she had done nothing wrong.

When Mr. Blue saw Gwen standing over Gertie who was sprawled in the dirt, he didn't hesitate. He grabbed her by her ear and pulled her home. Her mother and sisters had come out of the church to see what happened and they followed along behind them. Their three brothers would have to represent the family in church that morning.

When they got back to the house, their mother sat them all down in the parlor. "I want to know what on earth is going on with you! All of you!"

Gwen crossed her arms over her chest. "Gertie admitted that she started the rumors. I know it's not ladylike to hit someone, but sometimes I think that justice is more important than being ladylike."

Mrs. Blue looked at Gwen and shook her head. "I have to disagree, if you're hitting someone on church grounds during Sunday morning service! What were you thinking?"

Mr. Blue glared at his wife. "She's obviously thinking that you're going to let her get away with whatever she does like you always have. You have turned all three girls into little snobs. Gwen runs around with a different man every other week. We heard she was in trouble, and we both believed it! That tells me there's a problem right there. No more. I'm going to find husbands for all three of them."

Gwen jumped out of her chair. She'd always been the most vocal of the three. "I won't do it! You can't make me marry someone I don't want to marry! What are you going to do? Lock me in my room?"

Mr. Blue's face turned red with anger. "That's exactly what I'm going to do. You have been out of control for too long. From now on you will take all of your meals in your room. You may come out to use the water closet, but only if your mother or I accompany you." He grabbed her by her upper arm and dragged her up the stairs to her small room.

Gwen threw herself on her bed and sobbed loudly, knowing her mother would never hold out against her sobs. She never had, and she never would.

Libby and Bonnie sat in the parlor with their mother listening to Gwen's wails. "Mama, you can't really let Papa lock Gwen up until she marries," insisted Libby. "Can you?"

Mrs. Blue shrugged. "I have no control over him. He's my husband. I was taught to honor and obey my parents *and* my husband. I should have taught you three girls to do the same thing." She shook her head. "I'm afraid I'll have to let your papa do whatever he thinks is right this time."

Libby and Bonnie exchanged a look. "Would it be all right if we went in to talk to her?" Bonnie asked. She had an idea, one that she'd been formulating for a while, and she needed to talk to her sisters about it.

Mrs. Blue eyed her eldest daughter for a moment before shaking her head. "I don't think that's a good idea. I don't trust you girls not to let her out."

"But…you can't think to keep us apart for as long as it takes to plan a wedding! That's ridiculous." Libby couldn't believe her mother would even think of doing such a thing.

Bonnie reached over and squeezed Libby's hand, her way of signaling that she had an idea.

Mrs. Blue sighed. "I don't know what we'll do. I just know I'm not going to fight with my husband about the punishment you girls have been given. I'm done protecting you from him. After today, I'm done helping you at all. You all shamed me today."

Libby shook her head. "No, Mama. Only Gwen shamed you. We were good."

Mrs. Blue was startled by that for a moment. "Oh, you were. It was only Gwen, wasn't it?"

"I think we'll go up to our room now." Bonnie got to her feet and looked at Libby, letting her know without a word that they had some serious talking to do.

Gwen had always had her own room because she was too bossy to share with her sisters. They liked their room more orderly than she did, and her response was always, "Clean up my stuff yourself then." It worked out better for everyone.

As soon as they reached their room, Bonnie closed the door. She got something out of her dresser drawer and sat down on the bed. Once Libby was sitting in front of her, she handed her the letter she'd gotten.

Libby looked down at the letter. "What's this?"

Bonnie shrugged. "Libby, we both know I have no future in Beckham. Next to you and Gwen, I'm the ugly duckling. Goodness, everyone calls me 'Scrawny Bonnie' behind my back, don't pretend they don't. I've never had a single suitor, while you both have had plenty of men interested in you — and I'm the oldest! I'm twenty-three and an old maid."

Libby started to protest but Bonnie interrupted her. "I've come to terms with it, Libby. But that doesn't mean I don't want to marry. Unlike you and Gwen, though, I don't subscribe to the fantasy that I will only marry for love. A business arrangement would suit me just fine, so I spoke to Elizabeth Miller, the lady who runs the mail order bride agency."

Libby gasped at that. "Did you get a proposal? Are you leaving us?!"

"Read the letter," Bonnie murmured.

Libby read it and looked up and her sister, confused. "But this letter is looking for three women, not one."

Bonnie nodded. "I was going to talk to a couple of other unattached friends my age but... Libby, we need to leave town as soon as possible. Did you see the look in Papa's eyes? He's really going to marry us off, and I suspect it's to that trio of creepy old deacons from church he's been speaking with every Sunday. I couldn't stand that humiliation.

"No! Not them! He wouldn't dare! I'm only eighteen! Mother wouldn't let him."

"Didn't you hear her? She won't protect you and Gwen anymore, Libby. I know that's hard to hear since she's spoiled you two so much, but I can tell you from experience, that when she gives up on you, it's forever."

Libby had a pained look on her face as if she was trying to figure out a puzzle. Bonnie knew to just wait. Sometimes it took her beautiful sister a little bit longer to catch on, but she always did...eventually.

"So instead of marrying those old lechers, we run away to Texas and marry strangers?"

"At least they're young strangers, Libby. We can start completely from scratch without anyone knowing about this ridiculous scandal. Even if Papa doesn't force us to marry his friends, no one else will want us for a very long time, if ever."

Libby gave Bonnie a sly look. "Do we have to take Gwen?"

Bonnie smiled. "She may be annoying, but she's our sister. She probably needs this more than either of us. Let's rescue her from herself, Libby. What do you say?"

After a moment Libby nodded. "Let's make it happen."

ONE

Beckham, Massachusetts, October 1888

"Thank you, Mrs. Jamison! Thank you very much!" Libby Blue called over her shoulder as she left the dressmaker's shop. When she reached the street, she counted the coins in her hand before putting them in her reticule. When added to the rest of the money she'd collected over the last couple of weeks, there'd be quite the sum.

"Ten dollars," she whispered. A small fortune to be sure, at least to Libby, but would it be enough? Her older sister, Bonnie, put Libby in charge of gathering the funds they would need for her plan to work. A plan to keep Libby, and her two older sisters, from marrying three men their father chose for them in his haste to remedy a scandal brought on by Gwen. Unfortunately, his choices were elderly, pompous deacons of the church, and, unbeknownst to him, greedy and lecherous. This didn't set well with Libby or her sisters, and Bonnie, the oldest, quickly came up with a way to remedy the situation.

After a harrowing half-hour with their mother, Bonnie ushered Libby upstairs to their room and closed the door. She got something out of her dresser drawer and sat down on the bed. Once Libby was sitting in front of her, she handed her a letter. Libby recalled the conversation almost word for word. She remembered looking at the letter and asking,

"What is this?'

"Libby, we both know I've no future in Beckham," Bonnie said. "Next to you and Gwen, I'm the ugly duckling. Goodness, everyone calls me 'Scrawny Bonnie' behind my back; don't pretend they don't. I've not a single suitor, while you both have had plenty of men interested in you – and I'm the oldest! I'm twenty-three and an old maid."

Libby started to protest, but Bonnie interrupted her. "I've come to terms with it, Libby. But that doesn't mean I don't want to marry. Unlike you and Gwen, though, I don't subscribe to the fantasy that I will only marry for love. A business arrangement would suit me just fine, so I spoke to Elizabeth Miller, the lady who runs the mail-order bride agency."

Libby gasped at that. "Did you get a proposal? Are you leaving us?!"

"Read the letter," Bonnie murmured as she indicated the missive.

Libby read it and then stared at her. "But this letter is looking for three women, not one."

Bonnie nodded. "I was going to talk to a couple of other unattached friends my age but... Libby, we need to leave town as soon as possible. Did you see the look in Papa's eyes? He's going to marry us off, and I suspect it's to that trio of creepy old deacons from church he's been speaking with every Sunday.

I couldn't stand that kind of humiliation."

"No! Not them! He wouldn't dare! I'm only eighteen! Mother wouldn't let him!"

"Didn't you listen? She won't protect you and Gwen anymore, Libby. I know this is hard to hear since she spoiled you two so much, but I can tell you from experience that, when she gives up on you, it's forever."

Libby tried to grasp what Bonnie was saying. Against her will, her father was going to marry off not only Gwen, but Bonnie and Libby to the worst of men to keep a scandal at bay. "So, instead of marrying those old lechers, we run away to Texas and marry strangers?" she asked.

"At least they're young strangers, Libby. We can start from scratch without anyone knowing about this ridiculous scandal. Even if Papa doesn't force us to marry his friends, no one else will want us for a very long time, if ever."

Self-preservation hit, and forced Libby to ask, "Do we *have* to take Gwen?"

Bonnie smiled. "She may be annoying, but she's our sister. She needs this more than either of us. Let's rescue her from herself, Libby. What do you say?"

Gwen would have her pick of the men, which rankled. Libby would get second best; unless they were intellects, and then she'd get last. But which did she prefer? To be married to a man three times her age? Or a younger man who wanted a wife to start a life with? She stared at Bonnie. There was only one answer she could give. Escape was their only option. "Let's make it happen."

Libby smiled at the recollection, clutched her reticule to her chest, and hurried down the street. If she made more deliveries for Mr. Pomeroy at the bakery, he might give her the same amount of money Mrs. Jamison did this past week. If she'd been thinking, she'd have asked Bonnie how much they'd need for the upcoming journey, but was so intent on the task itself that the thought slipped her mind. Pleasing Bonnie mattered to her, and her sister would be happy with the amount Libby had collected. Her eldest sister's plan must work! If not, they'd be doomed to a life of... well, to be truthful, Libby wasn't sure what their lives would be like married to three old deacons. But she did know it wouldn't be pleasant. No, not pleasant at all.

The screams and wails of protest coming from Gwen's room were proof enough. Her father locked the poor girl upstairs after the scandal broke, and refused to let her out except to use the water closet. Now Gwen didn't even come out to do that. She started using a chamber pot instead. But what convinced Libby their circumstances were indeed dire was every time Bonnie talked about them, her face went pale with a hollow look, soon followed by a flash of anger in her eyes. Libby didn't blame her, not one bit. What right did their father have to marry them off to such hideous men?

But was Bonnie's plan any better?

Yes, they would escape their father's arranged marriages, but was marrying complete strangers the right way to do it? Did Bonnie even think when she set this up? But Libby learned long ago to listen to her sister, even though half the time, Bonnie didn't think she did. At this point, Libby thought Bonnie was smarter than their father. At least her eldest sister cared about her and Gwen. If their father cared even half as much as Bonnie, he wouldn't be marrying them off in the first place. His reputation was more important to him than his three daughters, and it hurt. Libby was glad she and her sisters were leaving Beckham to marry men of their choosing, and not their father's.

"Well, hello, Miss. Libby," called a familiar voice.

Libby turned and saw her brother Percy's friend, Samuel, approaching her at a rapid pace. What did he want? "Hello," she said as he reached her.

"Have you seen Percy?"

"He was home when I left."

Samuel glanced across the street. "What are you doing about town, and unescorted?"

"Running some errands. Now, if you don't mind, I'd best be on my way." She turned to leave.

He grabbed her arm. "How's your sister?" he asked with a grin.

"Which one?" But she knew he spoke of Gwen.

"Word is your father locked her in her room for a year."

"I think your hearing is off. Who locks a girl in her room for a year?"

"Your pa, that's who."

"You leave my father out of this. He... did what he thought was best... and besides, it wasn't Gwen's fault."

"Wasn't it?" he asked with a leer. "She did more than kiss Stanley."

"Who told you that? Anne Landry, I suppose."

"Your brother, Percy, if you must know."

Libby's mouth dropped open. "That's a lie!"

"And to think *you* kissed Stanley, too." He glanced around again, and took a step closer. "You can kiss me if you want, in the back alley behind the bank."

Libby gasped as her hand came up to slap him. He grabbed her wrist and held it fast as his eyes raked her over a second time. "If you change your mind, you know where to find me." He released her wrist, turned on his boot-heel, and walked away. Several townspeople stared at her and shook their heads, while making tsk, tsk sounds.

Libby swallowed hard in an effort to ignore them, clutched her reticule with both hands, and ran all the way to Pomeroy's Bakery.

Once inside, she peered out the windows to make sure Samuel hadn't followed her.

"What are you looking at, Miss Blue?"

Libby spun around. "Oh, Mr. Pomeroy... ah, nothing." She came away from the window and crossed the room to the counter. "I happened to be passing by, and wondered if you would like anything delivered this afternoon."

"Does your pa know you're making deliveries for me?"

"He won't mind," Libby said with a shy smile. "Father always says busy girls are better girls."

Mr. Pomeroy raised an inquisitive brow. "Yes, well, according to the local gossip mongers, your older sister's been busy indeed."

Libby fought against a groan. If one more person brought Gwen's supposed indiscretion up again... she thought she might scream! "I can assure you, sir, Gwen didn't do anything this time."

"Exactly. This time. She's done enough beforehand; no one believes her on this one. I hope you and your other sister learn by her mistakes."

"Gwen can't help it if she's beautiful, Mr. Pomeroy. All the boys flock to her; they always have."

"Yes, but she shouldn't take advantage of a man's admiration the way she does. It's going to get her nothing but trouble, and now it has."

"But, Mr. Pomeroy..."

"Don't try to defend her, just live and learn." He reached behind him and grabbed a small, wrapped cake box. "I need this delivered to the Thompsons, if you don't mind."

Libby's eyes lit up "Right away, sir," she said as she took the cake box from him.

"When you get back, I'll see if there's anything else for you to do, then it's straight home, or you'll be late for supper."

"Don't worry, Mr. Pomeroy. I'll hurry right back!" Libby left the bakery, a smile on her face. In a few days there'd be enough money to fund Bonnie's escape plan. If lucky, she'd be able to make this delivery without being stopped by some naysayer, determined to rub Gwen's discretions in her face. After this latest escapade, Libby didn't feel like trying to live up to her sister's beauty anymore. This time it caused Gwen nothing but trouble, and got her locked in her room to boot.

For as long as she could remember, Libby had lived in the shadow of her two sisters. She'd spent day after day trying to reach the same lofty heights they achieved. Gwen was the most beautiful of the three, the most beautiful in school and, if Libby thought about it, the most beautiful girl in Beckham. Too bad she was also one of the most annoying.

Where Gwen had beauty, Bonnie had brains. If someone could mold Gwen and Bonnie into the same person, they'd create someone downright dangerous. Libby wanted to be that person, and so, day in and day out, she tried to make herself beautiful like Gwen and smart like Bonnie. In secret, she read books from their father's small library in order to raise her intellect. So far all it had raised was her vocabulary, not to mention improved her spelling. But knowing a few fancy words couldn't help Libby measure up to her sisters' glorified status on either count. If reading Shakespeare's sonnets made Libby smarter, then *she* would've come up with a plan to save them from marrying three lecherous old men.

Nor did her attempts at beautifying herself land her a husband or more admirers. Her ardent admirers stayed only until they saw Gwen, and any further admiration for Libby was over. Bonnie's plan of escape appealed because, if Gwen were to marry, men wouldn't flock around her all the time. And if Bonnie married, she wouldn't be so worried *about* the men flocked around Gwen all the time. This, of course, meant Libby could stop trying to be like her sisters in order to catch a husband. Instead, via Bonnie's plan, she'd not only land a husband, but he wouldn't be a wrinkled old sour-puss who licked his lips every time he saw her.

Besides, with all the taunts Libby received while doing deliveries for Mr. Pomeroy and Mrs. Jamison, she was glad to leave Beckham. She'd get a fresh start in a new town, where no one compared her to Gwen and Bonnie. No longer would she listen to things like: "too bad your dress doesn't fit you as good as it does Gwen." Or, "why can't you be more like Bonnie and think for a change?"

But Bonnie's magnificent mind failed to catch her a husband, so Libby tried harder to be more like Gwen. However, whereas being beautiful came easy to Gwen–simply because she was–it wasn't so easy for Libby. She fussed with her hair throughout the day, pinched her cheeks to keep them rosy, and did what she could to make her lips more appealing to the opposite sex. In the early stages of her sister's bedroom incarceration, Libby even wished that *she'd* caused the scandal instead of Gwen. But no, Gwen beat her to it.

Her life was quite pathetic when she thought on it, and so she tried not to.

She dropped off the cake Mr. Pomeroy gave her, returned to the bakery, collected more money, and made another delivery before she went home. When she got to the house, Samuel, who'd insulted her in the street earlier, was just leaving.

"And here she is now," he drawled as she came up the walk. Percival, the youngest of Libby's three brothers, stood behind him, glaring at her. Samuel noted his scowl, and smiled. "Old man Jackson is sure lucky to be marrying your sister."

Percy ignored his comment, and instead shoved him out of the way. "Where have you been? It's bad enough the whole family comes off bad because of Gwen, but now you and Bonnie are out running around town half the day."

"I was not 'running around' I had errands to do,"

said Libby as she made to push past him.

Percy grabbed one arm as Samuel grabbed the other. "Mother isn't happy you've been out," he informed her.

"She was doing errands, Percy," Samuel said in her defense. "I know because I ran into her while looking for you."

Libby wrenched her arm out of Percy's grip, and tried to do the same with Samuel. Like before, he wouldn't let go. She grimaced. "Do you mind?"

"Not at all," he said and leered at her.

Percy's eyes narrowed. "Take your hand off my sister."

Samuel laughed. "What do you care? One's as good as the other."

Percy grabbed Libby's arm and pulled her out of Samuel's grip. "What is that supposed to mean?"

"Come on now, Percy; I'm sure your little sister wouldn't mind taking a stroll with me. Gwen sure didn't."

"Gwen never took a stroll with you," Percy hissed.

"No, but she did with Stanley. But never mind Gwen; she's not for me. I'd rather take Libby, here."

Percy shoved Libby into the house with one arm as he pulled back the other. The blow he delivered Samuel made a sickening crunch, and Libby yelped in surprise as her brother's friend dropped like a stone. "No one talks about my sisters like that!"

Samuel groaned as he pushed himself up on his elbows and shook his head. "What did ya do that for? Especially after all your talk about Gwen being an idiot for what she did with Stanley!"

"My sister's an idiot for letting people *think* she

did what she didn't do!"

"What?" Samuel asked, confused, as he rubbed his jaw and struggled to his feet.

"Oh, never mind!" said Percy as he balled his hand into a fist again. "Just get out of here and leave my sister alone."

"Fine!" Samuel spat. "Some friend you are!" He turned on his heel and stomped down the front walk.

Percy let go a weary sigh as he watched him slam the gate and disappear down the street. He turned to Libby. "Are you all right?"

"Yes," she said in a weak voice. "I guess so."

Percy shook his head, put his hands on his hips, and glared at her again. "If only Gwen hadn't... I mean, if you had any sense at all... and what are we going to do about Bonnie?!" he groaned and threw his hands in the air. "I'll be glad when this is all over!" He pushed past her and headed for the staircase, muttering the whole time.

Libby peered down the walk. Samuel was nowhere to be seen. She stared at the staircase in the hall. Percy had vanished as well. Closing the door, she smoothed the skirt of her dress, held her head high, and went up the stairs to her room to hide the money she'd made.

Upstairs, she stopped at her room and peeked inside. Empty. Percy hadn't been kidding when he said Bonnie was gone, too. But where had she gone? Libby turned and gazed across the hall at the door to Gwen's room. By now, she was used to seeing it shut and locked, and no longer cringed at the sight. She even missed Gwen yelling at her for barging into her room unannounced like she always did. Now no one but their mother went into Gwen's room, and lately it was to dump the chamber pot. What could Gwen be doing in there all this time? Did she even want to leave it? Maybe their mother wasn't letting Gwen use the water closet any more as a form of punishment. Libby gasped at the thought and went into her room.

Once inside, she closed the door and listened to make sure no one else came up the stairs. Convinced all was quiet, she went to her dresser and opened the top drawer. Libby took out a balled up pair of stockings she'd hid in the back, unrolled it, and emptied her reticule into one. She then rolled the stockings up and shoved them into the back of the drawer once more. Mr. Pomeroy had given her more than she'd thought, so now their total was ten dollars and twenty cents! Bonnie's plan was moving along perfectly, and soon the three sisters would leave Beckham. As far as Libby was concerned, they couldn't leave soon enough.

TWO

***The Dalton Ranch near Wiggieville, Texas,
November 1888***

Nate Dalton shoved his new sideboard against
the wall of the dining area of his small cabin. He
and his brother, Bart, had arrived in the late spring
and had gotten right to work building their tiny
castles of logs and mud. The structures weren't
much on the outside, but Nate, at least, was
determined to make things decent on the inside.
He'd worked for enough big spreads to develop a
hankering for the finer things, and spent all his
money on fancy furnishings for his tiny hovel. With
the stove Walton ordered for each of them, his cabin
was now complete. Consisting of two rooms, the
dwelling did indeed seem like a castle. Most folks
only had one.

With fists on hips, he surveyed his domain. A
settee and two chairs, with a table in between,
graced the living area in front of the fireplace. The
dining area consisted of the stove, sideboard, table,
and not two, but *four* chairs (in case he entertained),
with a small worktable tucked into a corner. He

planned to put in a dry sink one day, like if he got married in a year or two. For now, he didn't need one.

He'd built a small bookcase and placed his masterpiece near the bedroom door. Unable to help himself, he strolled across the cabin and gazed at his costliest extravagance, a brass bed. He'd picked it up in Weatherford the week before, and deemed the bed the best purchase he'd ever made. He'd never slept better in his life.

Of course, considering what he did for a living, a good night's sleep made all the difference. Working with cattle all day took a toll on a man, and quick. For the times he didn't make it home after days of watching over the Dalton herds, his new acquisition was gonna come in mighty handy. He'd even purchased a quilt from some church ladies in the nearby town of Wiggieville. The multicolored spread lit up the room and made things downright cheery. Nate smiled, pleased with himself.

He returned to the kitchen area and, taking a box from the table, took out what few dishes he owned and stacked them on the sideboard. Later he supposed he'd get more, but for now, he needn't worry. One man didn't need a lot of dishes to get by. As far as cookery, he had a coffee pot and a good, sturdy frying pan. They would be enough.

Nate stretched, admired his home one last time, and set out. He needed to check the stock in the south pastures, before driving to Weatherford with Walt and Bart to meet some cattle buyers. Walt said he'd struck a deal to benefit all three of them. Walt could be pretty savvy when it came to business dealings, which meant Nate didn't have to. He'd done his fair share over the years, and was happy to let someone else take charge for a change. He'd rather see to the cattle, and not deal with ranchers who always tried to undercut him, or cattle barons too big for their britches. Men of their ilk irritated him to no end, and were a constant reminder of why he preferred a saddle over a desk.

If Walt had his way, however, their ranch would grow by leaps and bounds, and in a few years Nate might yet find himself behind a desk. But Walton would take care of things for now, and Nate welcomed him to it. Bart, the youngest of the three triplets, felt the same.

Speaking of Bart, where was he? Of course, Nate knew Bart was always late. To *everything*!

Two hours later, Nate returned. "I hope Bart remembers to show up," he muttered as he headed to the barn to hitch up his buckboard. Walton had insisted they each bring their own, which made Nate wonder as to what kind of business deal Walt had gotten them into. But his older brother never steered him or Bart wrong, so Nate did what Walt wanted and, within minutes, his wagon was hitched up and ready to go.

"Bart's late," Walton announced as he strolled across the barnyard to Nate's buckboard.

"He's always late," Nate told him. "Especially when he's out *on safari.*"

Walton smiled. "Yeah, but for once I hope he breaks his record."

Nate laughed. "Not likely. He loves the wild too much. But don't worry; I'm sure he'll catch up." The youngest of the three, Bart called his outings on prairies and into the hills, safaris. At first, Nate thought him silly before he realized why Bart took off so often. How could he not? They now lived in God's country.

"You're right; he will," agreed Walt. "Let's go."

Nate watched as Walton strolled to his own wagon, climbed up and, with a slap of the reins, sped off. The drive to Weatherford took three hours on average, which made for small snippets of conversation between the two. Because they drove the wagons in single file, they shouted over the jangle of the harnesses to talk. But Nate didn't mind; he wasn't much of a talker anyway. In fact, he often preferred a good book to social gatherings, which was why he'd rather be out on the prairie with thousands of cattle; he didn't have to talk to them if he didn't want to.

When they reached Weatherford, Walt didn't drive to the stockyards as Nate had expected. Instead, he went straight to the train station. "What are we doing here?" he asked his older brother.

Walton gave him a huge grin. "You'll see."

Nate knew that grin. *Uh oh...*

"Trust me, brother, this is one of the best deals I've ever made," Walton said, his grin still in place.

"Who did you say we're meeting?"

"I didn't."

Nate stared at him as his mind raced. *Did* he tell them the cattlemen's names? He only remembered the part about a business deal, one to change their lives in a big way. Nate had assumed that meant obtaining more cattle. He'd thought the reason they each needed to bring a buckboard was to get supplies for a new barn or some such thing. More cattle meant more men and horses to tend them. Is that why they were at the train station, to pick up extra workers?

Before he could ask, a train whistle blew. Nate sighed. He might as well wait and find out what Walt had up his sleeve. So far, everything his older brother had done since Nate and Bart had arrived in Texas was to their benefit. So why would this be any different?

The two men parked their buckboards, climbed down, and then jumped up on the platform to await whatever the train carried.

The iron horse came to a screeching stop as the whistle blew a second time, loud and clear. Nate turned to check the horses, fearing the animals might become spooked by the noise.

"Don't worry, they're fine," said Walt as he eyed the train in anticipation.

Nate followed his gaze, his own surge of excitement going up his spine. The conductor got off first, and then walked down to the passenger car to help the people disembark. A few men stepped off, followed by several women. Walt slapped Nate on the arm. "Are you ready?" he asked him with a smile.

"As ready as I'll ever be. Where's Bart?"

"If he's not here, that's his problem. Means we get first pick."

"First pick?" Nate echoed as Walton made a direct path through the growing crowd. "Wait a minute," Nate said as he caught up to him. "What do you mean, first pick?"

Walton ignored him and continued on toward

three women huddled together on the platform. One of them, a beautiful blonde, looked annoyed. Another, a brunette, appeared more nervous, and the third, a homely thing, stood stiff, as if to keep herself in check. "Are you ladies the Blue sisters?" Walton asked.

The blonde gawked before she glared at him and nodded. "Who are you?"

"I'm Walton Dalton, and I pick you."

Nate watched in shock as Walt grabbed her hand and pulled her into his arms. She opened her mouth to protest, and his wily brother kissed her before she uttered a word.

What the heck?

The blonde stomped on his foot for his trouble. "Unhand me!"

Nate stood speechless as Walt smiled down at her. "I'll unhand you for now. Preacher's standing by."

"Preacher?" Nate whispered to himself. "What preacher?"

"Which sister are you?" Walt asked her, without relinquishing his hold.

"I'm Gwendolyn. Why do you persist in touching me? I don't know you!"

A good question; Nate wondered the same thing himself. Sure his brother had the same drive and hunger as the next man to bed a woman. But why on earth did he grab the girl and kiss her like that?

The homely-looking one came forward. "I'm Bonnie. I'm the oldest sister. I believe I'm the one you're supposed to marry."

Nate's mouth fell open in shock, but no one paid him any mind. "Ma ... ma ..." Dagnnabit!

Flabbergasted, he couldn't speak the word! *Married?*

Walt's eyes darted between the two sisters. "I don't care who's oldest. I'm marrying this one." He nodded at Nate, pulling him from his stupor. "That's my brother, Nate. Bart's not here now, but I'm sure he'll be along."

Nate stood and stared at the women and Walt in open-mouthed shock. Bart better be along! If he and Walt were in cahoots, he was going to kill them both!

The one called Bonnie glared at Walt a moment before she turned her death stare on Nate, whose eyes shifted to the brunette for safety's sake. But he *felt* Bonnie's gaze on him, as if daring him to turn and meet it. "Libby's the youngest," she said as if announcing an important piece of information.

Nate shook himself, and glanced between Walt and the one with the death stare. *What in Sam Hill were they talking about?* "I thought we were here to see about some cattle," he stammered.

Walt gave him his signature grin. "Surprise! Since Bart isn't here, you get next pick. Which one do you want for your bride?"

Nate blinked once, twice. What he wanted at this point was a drink. Had he heard him right? Walt couldn't … *he wouldn't* … would he? "You sent off for *brides* for us? The cattle salesman was a *lie*?"

Walt shrugged. "I didn't think you'd come if I told you why we were really here." He kissed the blonde on the top of her head, furthering his claim. "Pick one."

Nate seethed, and before he could stop himself— or for lack of a better idea—he pointed at the brunette. What was her name again? "I guess I'll take the youngest." Despite making a choice, this didn't mean he wasn't still mad as a rattler. He leaned toward Walt, his eyes narrowed to slits. "I'll take care of *you* later."

The blonde gasped. "You can't just pick me and say you'll marry me. No! What on earth is happening here? Bonnie? What have you done?"

That's what I'd like to know! Nate thought, too angry at this point to speak.

The woman in question blinked a few times in confusion. She looked like she was ready to cry. "Libby knew why we were here…"

Ah, yes, that's the girl's name…

"…we just didn't want you to be stubborn. We rescued you, after all."

Rescue? What rescue? Nate folded his arms across his chest, sensing a battle coming.

"Rescued me? You kept me from marrying a crazy old man, yes, but he was at least someone I knew! Now you expect me to marry a total stranger? He has a stupid name!"

Nate jerked at the statement. *Ouch.* He glanced at his brother, who looked as equally perturbed.

"I can't marry a man named Walton Dalton!" she prattled on. "Who would name their child that? What if he thinks we should name our child Dalton Dalton, or something?"

Nate saw Walt bristle. He'd always been a little sensitive about his name. The little chit was in for it now. "You're my bride," he told her. "You have no right to be making fun of my name like that. My pa's name was Alton, and he wanted to have another special name like that for me."

Gwen, was that her name, turned on him, her face red with anger. Nate leaned on one foot and studied the brunette again. *Hmmm...* He had to admit, she *was* pretty, what with her cream-colored skin, dark curls, and blue eyes.

"Special?" Gwen snapped pulling his attention away from his so-called bride. "You think your name is special? Well, let me tell you, it's not. It's just plain silly. I can't marry a man who has such an awful name. Find someone else!"

Nate pressed his lips together to keep from laughing. His earlier shock changed to amusement as he watched the two combatants go at it.

Walt's expression turned devilish. Nate knew the look. The woman didn't stand a chance. His brother gripped her shoulders and leaned down until they were eye to eye. "I've found my bride. We're marrying today. Don't make me take you over my knee as soon as we get home."

Nate put a fist to his mouth to keep from exploding into laughter. The sudden shock on the blonde's face was priceless.

She screeched something about threats, and then bombarded him with talk about visiting a friend from school. But when she said, "I had no idea the real reason I was brought here was to marry a stranger! You can't blame me for getting angry about that," he blanched.

She did have a point and, Nate had to admit, he agreed with her. Walt had tricked him, and Bart, if his guess was right, just as this woman's sisters had tricked her.

Walt shrugged. "Maybe I can't get angry for that, but I can certainly be mad at you for the way you're talking to me. I didn't trick you. Your sister did. Take it out on her."

Nate watched the eldest, Bonnie, and wondered what she would do. Meanwhile, Gwen stood and glared at the lot of them. "I'll be back." She turned and stomped down the platform. Walt stood a moment in indecision, before he took off after her.

Nate watched him go. He didn't envy the woman when he caught up to her. Walt could break anything. A horse, a dog, he even got a chicken to mind him once. But Miss Blondie was going to put his brother's skill to the test.

"I'm sorry your brother didn't tell you about us."

"Huh?" Nate said as his attention was pulled to the eldest sister. "Oh, yeah. Walt's like that."

"You ... you do still want to marry my other sister, don't you?"

"Look, uh ..."

"Bonnie," she said. "And this is Libby."

His gaze drifted back to the small brunette. She looked frightened and excited all at once. "Bonnie. It's not that I haven't thought of taking a wife. I just didn't plan on taking one today."

"I understand how you must feel."

"Do you? How long have you and Walt been planning this?"

"Ever since Gwen ..." Her sister, Libby, kicked her in the shin. "Ouch!"

Nate raised a curious brow and looked from one sister to the other. "Well?"

"Mr. Dalton, we've come a long way. We're tired, and we're hungry. The least you could do is..."

"Say no more. I've a little jerky in my wagon. Would you like some?"

They both gawked at him. Didn't they know what jerky was? "Thank you," they said in unison.

He nodded, almost afraid if he left them alone for a second, they'd bolt and run. But, wouldn't it be more of a relief? Why worry about them in the first place? He went to the wagon, dug into a small bag of supplies he always kept there, and pulled out a few pieces of jerky.

When he returned, the two women sat on the platform's only bench. "Here; it's not much, but it will tide you over for awhile."

"What's a while?" Libby asked, speaking for the first time.

He stared at her. He'd always like redheads, but he could get used to a brunette. "If my guess is right, we'll be making a trip to the preacher's house as soon as Bart gets here."

"And he's to be Bonnie's groom?"

Nate swallowed hard. "Yes," he managed. Why did this little thing affect him like this?

Good grief, if a strong enough wind came along, she'd blow away! He shook himself and forced his eyes in the direction of her sister, Bonnie. "Bart's a good man, you'll see. In fact, we're all good men, if you don't mind me saying so. We don't cuss much, drink only when we have a mind to, and are hard workers."

"Does this mean you're working hard to get used to the idea we're here?" the little brunette asked.

Nate swallowed again. His heart began to pound in his chest and, for the first time in a long time, he felt a pang of longing. Because of his brother's initiative, he'd be taking this pretty little thing home with him as his bride. "I think I'm getting used to the idea."

Bonnie sighed in resignation as she chewed on her jerky. "I'm glad to hear it."

He nodded, not knowing what else to do, and sat next to his intended. "Libby …"

"Yes?" she breathed.

"I was seeing how it sounded when I say it."

She gazed at him, wide-eyed, and a little embarrassed. "I'm sorry, but what's your name again?"

He coughed, and almost fell off the bench. She forgot his name, too? He bit the inside of his cheek to keep his anger in check. He wanted to kill Walt for this, but at the same time, he wanted to thank him for the craziest day of his life! "Nathanial, Nate, for short."

"Nate …" she repeated in a soft voice. "I think I like it." She swallowed hard and took her sister by the hand.

Her sister sighed again, and this time, Nate could tell it was out of relief. Maybe she was worried Libby wouldn't take to the idea of being a mail-order bride, and was worried she'd react the same way their sister, Gwen, had. He was about to say as much when Walt came back with his blonde goddess in tow, and not a moment later, Bart arrived.

Nate cringed. What was *he* going to think of all this?

THREE

Libby felt like a swarm of bees buzzed in her head. She and her sisters were really here! The train ride from Beckham had been torture. Gwen complained most of the way, and Bonnie—when she wasn't scolding them—would disappear for short bursts of time to leave them to fend for themselves. At first Libby labeled her a coward, and chalked up her frequent escapes to the back of the car as a way to free herself from Gwen's incessant talking. But, if she or Bonnie had been locked in their room for two months, they might be talking to make up for lost time, too. Libby was sure of one thing, though; if Gwen didn't stop harassing her about her cornflower-colored dress Libby had to leave behind, she was going to take advantage of Bonnie's disappearances and whack Gwen upside the head! Their older brother, Hank, used to do it to them all the time as children when he thought no one was looking, and got away with it. Why couldn't she?

The thought made Libby smile as she sneaked another peek at her intended. He was tall, much taller than she, but at five feet two-inches, that wasn't hard to do. Nate Dalton had to be at least six feet, as was his brother, Walt. The third brother, the one they were waiting for, must be the same.

She watched in silence as the two men spoke in low tones. Gwen still looked annoyed, and Bonnie … well, she looked like she'd just been asked to eat glass. Libby stared at her. She caught the look, gave Libby a gentle smile, and turned away. What was wrong? Wasn't Bonnie excited to be here? Hadn't they gotten everything sorted out with the two brothers, and now it was only a matter of waiting for her groom to show up?

He showed up all right…

Bonnie took one look at him, and went stiff as a board. She watched as Walt met him on the platform, spoke a few words, and then led him to the rest of their company. Libby couldn't figure out what her sister thought of the man she was to marry. He was no less handsome than his brothers, unless he had some horrible hidden deformity. Otherwise, he looked as good as the other men, which wasn't hard to do. They were identical triplets, after all.

But Libby sensed something wasn't right, and a cold shiver went up her spine. What if Bonnie didn't like him? What if she wanted to leave and go back to Beckham? What if that meant they still had to marry the deacons from he… Libby straightened. Polite young ladies didn't say, let alone think, those kinds of bad words.

But if Bonnie had a mind to go back, she knew that would be that. Judging from the look on Gwen's face, she'd be all for it. Libby swallowed hard. What to do? She liked her gentleman, even if he did scare her to death. She'd never had a serious beau. Once they got a gander at Gwen, they dropped her like a hot potato! She had to hang on to this one!

"Mr. Dalton?" she squeaked as she watched Bonnie and her Mr. Dalton step to one side of the platform. Oh no! What if she was telling him right this minute that it was no deal?

"Mr. Dalton?" she said a little louder, though it came out barely above a whisper.

"Yes?" he asked, as he also watched the couple converse, his brow puckered in concern.

"When are we to go to the preacher's house?"

"As soon as my brother gets over the shock, would be my guess." His eyes flicked to her. "I have to admit, I'm still trying to."

She sent Bonnie a worried glance, but she was busy speaking with her intended. Libby knew that look of hers, and knew whatever Bonnie was doing, she'd make sure it would work out. Bonnie always did. Why, then, did Libby feel so panicked?

She swallowed hard again, and gave Nate Dalton a shy smile. What if he changed his mind, but his brothers still married her sisters?! What would she do, then? A wave of dizziness struck, and she lurched to one side.

"Hey there, what's the matter?" Nate asked as he pulled her to him. "Are you okay?"

She gaped at him and shook her head. "I'm fine! Long train ride." She shot another glance at everyone else. Walt and Gwen were still intent on Bonnie and Bart. They must sense it, too! Oh, please, no!

Libby was pulled out of her panic by a strong hand on her shoulder. "Are you sure you're all right?"

She nodded, not knowing what to say. Other than: I'm fine, but for the fact that I'll die if my big sister spoils this for me!

"I'm sorry," he said in a low voice. "I guess a puny piece of jerky isn't enough to fill you up after your trip. I'll see you get something more substantial after the wedding."

"Wedding?" she croaked.

Their eyes locked. Heat pooled in her belly, and she couldn't help putting a hand on her stomach. What was that about?

A sudden "Whoop!" from Walt Dalton pulled her out of Nate's gaze. She turned, saw Bonnie and Bart embracing, and sighed in relief. "Oh, thank Heaven!"

Nate gave her a quizzical look, then smiled and sighed as well. "Looks like we're in business."

"Business?"

Nate smiled at her. "I hope you like cows."

Libby grimaced. "Oh, yes, you're ranchers. How could I forget?"

"Don't feel bad, sometimes I do the same thing." With that, he took her by the hand, and they went to join the others.

After further introductions were made between Libby, Gwen, and the newly-arrived Bart, the six departed for the preacher's house. Libby had been excited and scared all at once, up to this point. But now she felt as if she might lose her breakfast. Her stomach was in knots, and she felt as pale as Bonnie looked. Gwen— doggone her— still looked annoyed. Libby wished she felt annoyed. Anything would be better than the rising nausea she now battled. And she'd known what was coming! She couldn't imagine how she'd feel if she was in Gwen's position. She stared at her sister as she walked next to Walton in front of them. Gwen strode like a queen being paraded down the street. Libby could well imagine her expression, one that dared anyone to look at her, lest they have their head lopped off.

Libby sighed. How she envied her sister's confidence.

Before long they arrived at the preacher's, and Libby felt her palms begin to sweat. She chanced a peek at Nate, and noticed how tightly he held his jaw. Was he angry? Anxious? Having second thoughts?

She hoped it wasn't the latter, and that he was only nervous.

She wiped her palms against the skirt of her dress, and then balled her hands into fists as another chill went up her spine. Even after their long journey, she couldn't believe she was going through with this. Yet, she had to if she wanted to survive. Marrying Nate Dalton meant protection and provision, not to mention a chance at happiness. Of course, there was the fact that had she and her sisters stayed in Beckham, they'd be married to three old goats by now and doomed to live out their lives in misery. The mere thought made her tremble.

Nate bent to her. "You're shaking like a leaf. Are you all right?"

"I'm about to marry a complete stranger. How 'all right' are you?"

He let out a heavy sigh. "I understand. In fact, I'm not sure why I'm going along with this."

She glanced at him and caught the confusion in his eyes. She bit her lip to keep it from trembling, too. "Then why are you?"

He looked her up and down, his eyes finally settling on her own. "It's a funny thing, really, when Walt does things like this. Bart and I are compelled to go along. I can't explain why, we just do."

"If your brother stepped out in front of a train, does that mean you and your brother would do the same?" Her voice was terse, but his words stung. He made it quite obvious he didn't want to marry her. He was going to do it because it was his brother's idea, not his.

"We'd best go inside," he told her.

Libby glanced around and noticed the others heading up the front walk. She took a deep breath, closed her eyes in resignation for a second, and then let him lead her to the front door. Within moments, the three couples were ushered inside by the preacher's wife and, after brief introductions, the ceremony got underway.

Libby eyed Walt Dalton, who looked immensely pleased with himself at the moment, as if he'd just conquered the world. Gwen, God bless her, still looked annoyed! Libby would have to lean too far forward to catch a glimpse of Bonnie, and so, not wanting to bring attention to herself, remained where she was. She so wished she could see her sister's face and draw comfort from it. She knew if Bonnie was as nervous as she, she would never show it. Libby, however, could never hide her emotions, and this particular occasion was no different.

Her knees started to knock.

Nate stared straight ahead as the preacher droned on, but soon it became apparent, judging from his one raised eyebrow and the slow turn of his head in her direction, that she was causing a distraction. She forced a smile and tried not to throw up. She almost jumped when she felt her hand engulfed by his and he gave it a gentle squeeze. She relaxed a notch at his touch, and noticed how large his hand was. Even more so, she noticed how good his hand felt.

Within moments, the preacher stopped and looked at each of them in turn, and then began to recite their vows. As a young girl, Libby had dreamed of a big, beautiful wedding. She'd envisioned herself dressed like a princess, all in white. She even wore a tiara. Gwen and Bonnie would be her bridesmaids, and Adelaide Tompkins, her best friend in Beckham, her maid of honor. Her father would walk her down the aisle with pride, and her mother would cry her eyes out when he placed her hand into that of her intended's. They would face the preacher, say their vows and then…

"You may kiss your brides!"

Libby's jaw dropped like a brick. Good grief, had she even said, "I do?" She couldn't remember! She'd been so wrapped up in her wedding daydream, she wasn't sure if she was married. But then, Nate looked at her, really looked at her, took her other hand and pulled her around to face him. She was vaguely aware of Gwen's gasp as Walt grabbed her and kissed her with everything he had. She still couldn't see Bonnie, only Gwen's flaying arms waving behind Nate.

Was he going to kiss her like that? Was Bonnie, even now, trying to come up for air like Gwen? It was obvious her sisters' husbands were happy to have wives! But Nate Dalton stood stock-still, and stared at her a moment longer before he finally bent down and, ever so gently, brushed his lips across her own.

Libby's knees knocked again, but it wasn't because she was nervous. Instead, a delicious chill went up her spine and she stared at him, wide-eyed. She'd never been kissed before, and wasn't sure what to expect. But why hadn't he kissed her the same way Walt had kissed Gwen? She didn't see Bonnie and Bart's kiss, but was sure it had to be the same. Was Nate Dalton displeased with her? Did she repulse him to the point he could only muster up a mere peck?

Libby tried not to cry, and forced a smile instead. She may yet be faced with a loveless, miserable marriage, but with one difference; Nate Dalton, with his dark wavy hair and rich brown eyes, was easier on *her* eyes than the old deacon her father had picked out.

He was married.

Nate stared at his new bride in utter fascination. He supposed he should count himself lucky she was so pretty. She was also quite innocent, he could see it in her eyes, and knew the kiss he'd just given her was her first. True, he could've claimed her like Walt had done her sister, but he didn't want to frighten his new bride. If he did anymore than what he had, he feared she might break. Her delicate features and ivory skin reminded him of a China doll, which gave him second thoughts about the little thing being a good rancher's wife. But it was too late now. They were married.

Slaps of congratulations, handshakes with the preacher, and the faces of three women in shock, followed. Within moments they were preparing to depart for home, and Nate couldn't be more ready. He'd entered unfamiliar territory today, and wanted nothing more than to surround himself with the familiar. Besides, his curiosity was peaked. He didn't know this woman, and wondered how he was going to go about the task. Talking wasn't his strong point, and she seemed the type to need a lot of reassurance. She reminded him of a frightened animal, one that, if you didn't calm it down quick, would attack you.

This was going to be a long ride home.

Fortunately, the journey wasn't as bad as he thought. He offered up snippets of conversation, and at one point even made her laugh. Bart's new bride rode in the back of their wagon, and was amiable enough during the ride, and Walt… Well, Walt was Walt. He lit out of Weatherford as fast as lightning, and was the first to get home. Nate grinned as he drove. He didn't envy his big brother's new wife. She was going to be surprised when she learned she couldn't pull anything over on him.

Nate glanced at his own bride, and wondered if she had the same fire as her sister, or if she was more reserved like Bonnie. It was hard to tell. His little Libby had walls. He knew, if only because he had them himself. He'd been forced to build them long ago. What forced her to build the ones she had?

By the time they dropped Bonnie off at Bart's and reached his place, the sun had set and there were still chores to be done. He helped his bride out of the wagon and walked her to the door of her new home. Pride welled up within him as he gazed at her and smiled. "We don't have much yet," he told her, "but we will."

She stared off into the distance where they'd left her sister Bonnie. "They're so close," she breathed in disbelief. She looked at him, tears in her eyes, and smiled. "We're so close!"

"Yes, Walt wanted things that way. His cabin is over that way," he said and pointed. "You can see your sisters whenever you want."

She choked back a sob. It was all he could do not to take her in his arms and comfort her. Was she happy, or sad? He glanced at Bart's cabin, and knew she was happy to find her siblings were her neighbors. But were there other reasons she'd be crying?

He opened the front door and stared at her. "Should I carry you over the threshold? Isn't that how these things are done? Er...do you know?"

"Do I what?"

He scratched his head and shrugged. "I think I'm supposed to carry you into the house. It's customary."

Her eyes widened and she took a step back. "Are you asking… if I want you to?"

"Isn't that the polite thing to do?"

She closed her eyes and lowered her head so he couldn't see her face. The realization that he wanted to scoop her up and carry her into the house surprised even him. Unable to help himself, he reached out and put a finger under her chin, and then lifted her face so he could gaze into her eyes by the moonlight. When he did, he wished he hadn't. Libby Dalton, his new wife, looked as sad as sad could be.

FOUR

He didn't even want to carry her across the threshold? How pathetic was that? Libby bet Bonnie and Gwen were carried across their thresholds by their new husbands! Especially Bonnie, what with the way Bart held her at the train station. Maybe Bart waited until after she and Nate left to do it, but Libby knew he did!

But Nate Dalton? He wasn't so happy to be married.

Libby clenched her fists, stuck up her chin, and marched past him into the house. It was small, smaller than she'd expected, and even in the dim moonlight coming through the windows, she could tell there was no escaping the man she'd married. She'd trip over him in the small dwelling, and that would be on the good days. She swallowed hard and turned to face him.

He stood on the threshold and stared at her, his lips pressed into a firm line. "Right, then," he said, then turned on his boot-heel and retreated to the wagon. He removed her satchel, returned to the house, and set it on the kitchen table. At least, she assumed it was a table, judging from what little light there was. After he lit a lantern and hung it on a hook, she could see it was indeed a table. A very nice one, too, with a cheery tablecloth that made her mouth curve into a smile.

He studied her, and then glanced about the cabin. "I hope you find it to your liking," he said. "I'd best go unhitch the wagon and get a few chores done before supper." He walked past her to the door and stopped. "Can you cook?" he asked, without turning around.

Here it was, the moment of truth. If he'd found her lacking as a wife before, she had no doubt he'd regret his choice to marry her now. "No," she answered. "Not a whit."

Again, without turning, he spoke. "You'll learn." And, with that, he left the cabin and shut the door behind him.

Libby stood as an odd numbness took hold. He didn't want her, probably didn't need her. While her two sisters would no doubt be entering into marital bliss with their new husbands, she wondered if Nate would so much as utter a word to her. Ever. Lord knew he'd hardly done so on the wagon ride out. Why would she think he'd be any different once they arrived?

But now she was here, and very much married to him. All she could do was make the best of it, and be thankful her sisters were there to keep her company. At least *they* would be happy.

Libby let out a heavy sigh and studied her surroundings. A rock fireplace graced one wall of the cabin. A beautiful settee and two chairs sat in front of it. She walked to the area and smiled. For a rough and tough cowboy, the man had good taste.

Like the tablecloth, a cheerily colored rug lay between the fireplace and settee, and a small table had been placed between the two chairs. The area was big enough for a third chair opposite the two, which would turn the arrangement into a lovely conversation spot. She stepped back into the kitchen area and took in the large cook stove. It frightened her. How was she ever going to please this man, when he already found her so lacking? She pushed the thought aside and studied the sideboard, small worktable, and the rest of the cabin. She then noticed the door near a bookcase, and came to the conclusion that it must lead to the bedroom. "Oh, good heavens…" she muttered.

Gathering her courage, Libby crossed to the door, put her hand on the knob, and opened it. With a gasp, she stepped into the room. "Oh, my word; how beautiful!"

A brass bed sat against one wall. There was a trunk at the foot of it, with several neatly folded blankets at the ready. The bed itself was more than big enough for two people, and covered by one of the most beautiful quilts Libby had ever seen. An armoire took up one corner of the room, and a dresser with a mirror graced the opposite wall. The room itself was almost as big as the living area of the cabin, and Libby knew she would be spending a lot of time in the cheery bedroom, if only to escape her new husband's sour disposition. Speaking of which, how was she going to avoid him from now on? More importantly, how was she going to avoid him tonight? It was their wedding night, after all, and even though her mother had never spoken to her about what went on between a man and woman, she'd eavesdropped on her brothers often enough to have a good idea. None of it sounded pleasant, at least not if one was on the receiving end of things. Her brothers' descriptions were crude at best, and often quelled any further eavesdropping on her part. At least men enjoyed such things, but she doubted she would. This, of course, left her with one burning question. How was she going to avoid sleeping with her husband tonight?

Nate took care of the horses, fed the chickens, and was heading back to the house when he stopped dead in his tracks. What would happen now? She couldn't cook, was frightened and, as far as he knew, didn't like this whole arrangement. He stood, fists on hips, and stared at the soft lantern light coming from the windows. Maybe she was upset because she was so ill-prepared to be a wife. How would he feel if he was in her shoes? But then, what woman becomes a wife and doesn't learn how to cook? What else would she be inept at? What if she couldn't so much as mend a shirt, or wash it for that matter? He couldn't exactly send her back. But then, what if that's exactly what she wanted him to do?

Nate rubbed his chin with his hand. How to handle her was the question. Should he be patient, or tell her to get with it? Maybe a little of both? Yet, what right did he have to be so hard on her their first day as husband and wife? She did just travel over a thousand miles to get there and must be plumb tuckered out. If he was any kind of a gentleman, he'd get a tub ready for her, let her have her privacy, then after she felt better, he could see where they really stood. Yes, that's what he'd do. He wouldn't be surprised if he found her passed out from exhaustion.

Sure enough, when he entered the house she was curled up at one end of the settee, eyes closed, breathing steady and even. He studied her in the lantern light. How was he going to turn this delicate flower into someone capable of defending herself and their land if need be? This was still rough country, and he and his brothers could be gone long hours during the day. She'd be alone all that time, as would her sisters. They might have to do whatever was necessary to defend themselves. Could she shoot a gun? Could she, *would she*, shoot a man if she had to? He crossed to the stove and pushed the thought aside. He'd worry about teaching her how to shoot later. Right now, he figured he'd help make things more comfortable for her. Tomorrow was going to be a long day.

He got a fire in the cook stove going, fetched the tub he used for bathing, and set it up in the bedroom. He then went out to the pump, got a couple buckets of water, and poured them into the tub. He then filled the buckets again, and put them on the stove to heat.

While he waited, he sat at the kitchen table and stared at the back of the settee. He tried to imagine the two of them sitting there, in the evenings after supper in front of the fire. He'd read a book, she'd knit or something. After awhile, they'd maybe get sleepy; then again, maybe not. Nate swallowed hard, and stood. He took a few steps in her direction, and gazed at the back of her head resting on the one pillow he had for the living area. Her dark hair was coming loose from its pins; a long tendril had escaped, spilling over the arm of the settee. He went to her, reached down, and touched the silken lock. His body reacted, and he let go, sucking in a breath as he did. Libby didn't stir, and he sighed in relief.

Once again, he had to concede to her beauty. But how was she going to survive while he was gone all day? He didn't talk much during the ride home, but he listened. Her sister, Bonnie, had asked him if the land around Bart's home would support a vegetable garden come spring. He told her yes, and knew she wanted to have one so there'd be enough food to get them through next winter. She knew how to cook and preserve food, a good thing in these parts. Bart was one lucky son of a …

Libby moaned in her sleep. Nate froze. He sucked in another breath, and slowly backed away. He should wake her now, get her something to eat, and then leave her to bathe.

He went back to the kitchen. He had some cold bacon left from his breakfast, and a few biscuits. They would have to do for supper. He cut a biscuit in half, slapped a couple pieces of bacon on it, and then went to wake his sleeping wife.

He gave her shoulder a shake, and almost jumped when she popped up with a yelp. "Whoa, there," he said in a soft voice. "I didn't mean to scare ya."

She stared at him, her mouth half-open. "Wha… what?" She glanced around the cabin. "What happened?"

"You dozed off. Here, I rustled us up something to eat," he said and handed her the biscuit.

She looked at it, then at him. "What is it?"

"Just eat; you'll need something in your belly or you'll be worthless in the morning."

"Worthless?" she whispered. "I see." She took the biscuit from him, studied it, and took a small bite.

"I done fixed you a bath. You can get cleaned up before you turn in. I don't imagine you'd want to sleep in a clean bed unless you're the same."

She raised her eyes to his. "Understood," she said through gritted teeth.

Good grief! What was ailing her now? "I'll be out in the barn." He went to the stove, checked the water and, using a couple of dishrags, plucked the buckets off and added them to the tub in the bedroom. Maybe after she got cleaned up she wouldn't be so... well, whatever it was she was being! All he knew was he didn't care for it. If she was going to be the kind of woman who was hard to please, then this arrangement wasn't going to be to his liking; at least not until she learned what was what.

"I'm going to the barn. I'll be back in an hour." He didn't mean to slam the door on his way out, but he did. Some wedding night this was turning out to be.

Libby took a deep breath. The biscuit he gave

her was stale, but it was food, and she was hungry. She choked it down, surprised at how good a cold biscuit and bacon could taste, then got up and went into the bedroom to see what he'd done.

The room was bathed in the warm glow of candles and, just as he'd said, there was a tub of water. She peeked at it in the dim light to see how much water there was. Not much, but it would do in a pinch. Normally, she'd be thanking the Almighty for the steaming water but, under the circumstances, she wasn't too happy about his insult.

So, he feared she'd get his precious bed dirty, did he? Okay, maybe in her current state, he was correct. She hadn't had a decent bath in … good Lord, how long *had* it been?

Libby propped a chair under the doorknob, as she'd seen Gwen do when she had some juicy scrap of gossip or secret she was about to divulge to her and Bonnie. She then peeled off her day dress, corset, petticoats and chemise. She noticed a bar of soap and a towel laid out on the trunk at the foot of the bed. A small smile curved her mouth. What if he was just being thoughtful? But no, not after the remark he'd made about getting his bed dirty! Maybe she shouldn't bathe at all; that would show him! But the temptation of the warm water was too much, and she felt disgusting besides.

She took the soap, set the towel on the floor next to the metal tub, and then eased herself into it. The water wasn't hot, but it wasn't cold either. She washed herself as fast as she could, then her hair. Not an easy task. She didn't think to grab the pitcher off the washstand so she could use it to rinse her hair out. After a few minutes of spitting and sputtering, she stood, her body dripping, and reached for the towel.

She dried herself then groaned. "Oh no, where's my satchel?" Of course, she knew, on the kitchen table, right where he'd left it. She sighed, took one of the blankets off the trunk, wrapped it around herself and, after removing the chair and pressing an ear to the door to make sure she was alone, raced out of the bedroom to retrieve her satchel. "Oh!" she cried as she ran right into her husband. She hit him so hard she bounced off his chest and stumbled back a few steps. "What are you doing here?"

"I live here," he said as he took in her choice of attire. "Nice blanket."

"Leave, this instant!" she screeched. "You can't see me like this!"

His eyes roamed her face before exploring the rest of her. He swallowed hard, then snatched his hat off the table, turned, and went out the front door without another word.

Libby let out the breath she'd been holding. She hadn't heard him come in, and didn't hear anything before she opened the door. Her new husband must be light on his feet. She grabbed her satchel from off the table and hurried back to the bedroom. "The nerve of him!" she hissed as she tossed the satchel onto the bed, opened it, and pulled out a nightdress. Like her, it could do with a good washing, but it was all she'd brought, and was still cleaner than she had been. She pulled it on, took out her comb, ran it through her hair a few times, and then quickly braided it. With her luck, it would still be wet in the morning, but she didn't care. She eyed the bedroom door, and wondered if she should prop the chair against it, but didn't feel right doing so. It wasn't Nate's fault he'd startled her just now. It was hers, for rushing out of the bedroom the way she did. She was lucky she didn't lose the blanket in the process.

Yet ... what if he came into the bedroom later and wanted to ...

Libby gulped. "Please Lord, I'm not ready for such a thing," she whispered. "I want him to at least love me a little, before ... *that*."

Maybe then, she'd be able stomach it.

FIVE

A short time later, Libby awoke to someone pounding on the bedroom door. That someone, of course, was her husband. "Libby! Open this door!"

Libby bolted upright in bed, her eyes wide with fear. What to do? Should she let him in, or let the man keep pounding? What if he broke the door down? Then what would she do? For lack of a better idea, she yelled, "Go away!"

"Go?" he shouted from the other side. "I live here! What is *wrong* with you?"

Think, Libby think! "Er….ah… I'm not ready to sleep with you!"

There was a moment of silence, and then, "What the Sam Hill are you talking about? We're married!"

"I will not sleep with a stranger!" she yelled back.

"Stranger? How else are we going to get to know each other?"

Libby twisted the quilt in her hands and tried to think of what to say. "Well… if you want to sleep in the same bed with me then… you're just going to have to… to woo me first!"

Dead silence.

"Nate?" came out in a pitiful squeak. She stared at the door and cringed. His retreating boot steps on the other side of it answered her. He was gone.

Libby flopped against the pillows with a sigh of relief. "I am in so much trouble," she said to the ceiling. "He'll never forgive me for this." But what else was she supposed to do? The thought of a complete stranger putting his hands on her was too much. But had turning her new husband away on their wedding night been the right thing to do?

Libby sat up again. "Of course it was! Bonnie or Gwen would've done the same thing if they were me! Wouldn't they?" Libby honestly didn't know.

The next morning, Libby awoke after a fitful sleep, sat up, and rubbed her eyes. The chair was still braced against the door, the cabin quiet. Sunlight streamed through the window, and she wondered what time it was. But what did it matter? This morning she would have to face her new husband and explain herself. She'd spent half the night figuring out what to tell him, and hoped she'd remember the words.

Libby tossed back the covers, got up, and sought her clothes. Everything needed a good washing at this point, and she dreaded the thought of having to do laundry for herself; a task she had never done in her life. She realized last night that she'd have to learn quite a few things in order to please her new husband. The mere thought overwhelmed her, and she tried to think of something else as she approached the bedroom door.

With her heart pounding in her chest, she reached for the chair and removed it. Then, with a trembling hand, she grabbed the doorknob. Of course, she pressed her ear to the door first and listened for any sound coming from the other side. A lot of good that was going to do her; she hadn't heard Nate last night, what made her think she'd hear him this morning? Libby took a deep breath, held it, and let it out slowly. She then opened the door.

Nothing. No one. There wasn't a trace of Nate Dalton anywhere in the cabin.

Libby ventured out of the bedroom on tiptoe, as if Nate would suddenly pop out of some hidden corner. She sighed in relief when she realized she was alone, and took in the sight of the cabin in the light of day. There were two large windows on either side of the door, another between the cook stove and the sideboard, and then of course the one in the bedroom. The cabin's interior was just as charming in daylight as it was by lantern light. She hoped Nate would build a fire in the evening after supper, so she could see what it looked like. That is, if she wasn't spending the night in the barn. Who knew what he would do when he got home? He had to be out working already; where else would he be?

Libby glanced around, and noticed a note on the table set near a plate with a single biscuit on it. She went to the table and snatched up the note.

Dear wife,
Here's your breakfast. Have my lunch ready by noon.
Sincerely, Your Husband.
p.s. Tonight you can sleep on the floor or the settee, the bed is mine.

He was mad all right. She tossed the note onto the table and clutched her hands together in front of her. What was she going to do? Should she give in to his demands, or stand her ground? What would Gwen or Bonnie do? Libby squared her shoulders and stared down the biscuit. They'd stand their ground, of course! "I won't let him break me!" Libby cried with a stomp of her foot. "I won't."

There was a sudden knock on the front door. Libby jumped and yelped at the same time. Was it Nate? Had he come back to the cabin early? What would he do to her? How mad could he still be?

Her eyes darted to the living room. The pillow she'd used the night before during her brief nap lay on the floor with a blanket. Libby swallowed hard. He was plenty mad. But if that were true, why would he knock on the door of his own cabin?

"Who is it?" she called out.

"It's me, Bonnie!"

"Bonnie!" Libby breathed as she ran for the door. "Thank the Lord!"

Libby threw the door open and smiled with relief at her older sister. "Oh, I'm so glad it's you!"

"Why?" Bonnie asked as she peered into the cabin. "What's the matter?"

Should she tell her? What if she'd allowed Bart to have his way with her last night? Would Bonnie berate her for not doing her wifely duty? "Oh... nothing."

Bonnie eyed Libby a moment before she tried to look into the cabin again. "Have you had your breakfast?"

Libby stepped aside as her eyes darted to the

lone biscuit on the table. "Not yet, but I was about to."

Bonnie stood on the threshold and stared open-mouthed at the charming interior. "Libby! This is… is… beautiful!"

Libby smiled; at least something was going right this morning. "Thank you. Who would've ever thought a man could decorate so nicely?"

Bonnie bit her lower lip and sucked air through her nose. She was upset about something, Libby could tell. But she was upset, too, and hoped Bonnie wouldn't notice. "I came to fetch you," Bonnie said as she stepped into the cabin and continue to gawk. "I know you and Gwen can't cook well." She turned to Libby. "But you don't have to worry about a thing; I'm going to teach you both everything I know."

Libby let out the breath she'd been holding. She was more wound up than she'd thought. "Oh, Bonnie, thank you! I don't know what we'd do without you."

"Neither do I," Bonnie said with a wry smile. "But I'm sure you'd manage."

Libby smiled back and shook her head. "You know very well we wouldn't! I don't know who would falter first, me or Gwen. Thank you for coming to our rescue in this time of need."

Bonnie laughed at that, and gave her a hug. "Don't worry, you'll survive. Learning to cook and do laundry isn't going to kill either one of you… I hope."

"Gwen might put up a fuss."

"No doubt she will, but if the two of you don't learn how to take care of your husbands, your lives won't be very pleasant. These men are willing to protect and provide for us; the least we can do is protect and provide for them."

"For them?" Libby said. "I don't understand."

Bonnie shrugged. "They bring us the food, we prepare the food. They protect us, and we protect them."

"How do we protect them?" Libby asked, still confused. What was her sister talking about?

Bonnie's expression became pained. "We guard their hearts, silly. It's what a woman does for a man."

"Who told you that?" Libby asked. She'd never heard anything of that nature come out of their mother's mouth.

"Elizabeth told me."

"You mean from the mail-order bride service?"

"Yes," Bonnie said, a solemn look on her face.

Libby shook her head again. "I still don't understand."

"I don't think a woman does until after she's been married awhile. I'm sure in time you and Gwen will get the hang of it."

"Me and Gwen, what about you?"

Bonnie's eyes widened a second, before she smiled. "I'm sure I will, too. Now, hurry and eat your breakfast. We need to get over to Gwen's. I have a lot to teach you this morning."

Libby grabbed the stale biscuit to munch on as she and Bonnie walked to Gwen's. When they arrived, they were both surprised to find their sister doing the dishes. Well, Libby was surprised; Bonnie looked incredibly pleased. "I see you're almost finished with those," Bonnie told Gwen. "I came over to bake bread for the next two days. You two need to learn to cook as soon as you can, so you can please your husbands."

Libby cringed. She certainly hadn't done well on that score yet. So far, all she was good at was making Nate angry. But with Bonnie's help, she might be able to waylay his anger long enough to figure out how to not only apologize for last night, but explain to him why she'd done what she'd done. She needed to feel he cared for her first, even if only a little. The desire was so strong, even she didn't understand it, nor where it came from. She only knew she wanted to matter to him, more importantly his heart, before he took her body. If he didn't care for her, she feared she'd go through life feeling like nothing more than chattel.

Gwen finished up her dishes. "Well? What happened last night? How do you like your new husbands?" She looked at Libby over her shoulder. "How did you and Nate get along?"

Libby closed her eyes a moment then opened them. She was going to have to fess up. She was sure Nate's brothers would sense something was wrong with him, and ask Nate about it. Better her sisters heard things from her now, than their husbands later. "Nate is angry with me for refusing to share the marriage bed with him." She raised her chin. "I made him sleep on the floor. I told him, he'd have to woo me."

Bonnie stared at her in shock as Gwen turned an

interesting shade of red. Libby almost kissed her when, after she put the last dish in a cabinet, she hurried to the table and sat. "I want to know everything there is to know about cooking!"

Libby let go a sigh of relief. Thank heavens they wouldn't ask her any questions! She didn't have any answers anyway.

They spent the rest of the morning preparing bread dough and, once Bonnie was satisfied they had enough, set bowls of the gooey stuff off to the side so the dough could rise. Gwen, exhausted, asked Bonnie what they would make the men for lunch, but Bonnie told her they were all on their own. Libby thought Gwen might faint when Bonnie said it, but quickly recovered as she and Bonnie left Gwen's cabin.

"Do you have anything to make for Nate's lunch?" Bonnie asked once they were outside.

"I have no idea," said Libby. And she didn't. She didn't even know if the man had a larder or where he kept anything.

"See what you can find. I'm sure Nate will appreciate anything you prepare for him."

Libby blanched as she walked, her next words coming out a croak. "I'll do my best."

Bonnie stopped and looked at her. "Is something wrong?"

Libby bit her lip, thinking fast. "I have a hungry man coming home and nothing to feed him."

"You're going to have to get used to this, Libby. Trust me, once you learn how to cook, sew, do the mending, clean, and... well... once you learn all those things and get good at them, he'll adore you."

"What if I didn't know how to do all those

things? What would make him adore me then?"

Bonnie stood silent for a moment, staring at her. "You're a beautiful girl, Libby. How could any man not adore you?" She turned away, and Libby swore there were tears in her eyes. But why? She blinked her own eyes a few times. Perhaps she was seeing things.

They reached Libby's cabin and Bonnie gave her another hug. "Good luck," she told her. She then spun on her heel and strode toward her own humble abode.

Libby put her hand on the knob and stared at the door. "He's not going to like this," she said as she opened it and went inside. With any luck, she'd find more stale biscuits. If not, she had no idea what she was going to do.

As it turned out, there wasn't a biscuit in sight, and Libby began to panic. "I can't believe a man of his size hasn't a scrap of food in this place!" She continued to search the kitchen, but all she turned up were a few jars. One with flour, another sugar, and the smallest held salt. "Now what am I going to do?" She tapped her foot on the floor a few times, her arms folded across her chest in frustration.

"I know!" she cried in excitement as her eyes lit with an idea. She hurried out of the cabin and walked around to the back. Sure enough, there was a small shed. It had to be a smokehouse! She turned and noted a small door at the back of the cabin. Could that be a root cellar? She didn't know which one to explore first. She finally settled on the smokehouse, where there would be more light to see by. It took her a moment to figure out how to open the door, but once she did, she sighed in relief at what she found. There was enough meat inside to last a month or more. She grabbed some sausages, as she figured they'd be the easiest to cook up, and headed back to the cabin. She stopped and stared at the small door in the back, and then took a deep breath to bolster her courage. A root cellar would be dark, and possibly full of... Libby shivered... spiders.

But wasn't pleasing her husband, as Bonnie said, worth a run-in with a few spiders? Libby didn't think so, but her sister would. "I'll do it for Bonnie!" Libby said to herself. "Be brave, Libby, be brave!" Gripping her sausages like they were a couple of billy clubs, she strode toward the door with determined steps. She swallowed hard, undid the latch, and slowly opened the small door. Crude steps led down into a cold, dark void. Libby went pale. "Oh, my goodness," she muttered as she took a step forward then froze. "I can do this, I can... I can't!" She slammed the door closed then ran for the front of the cabin.

Ashamed of herself, Libby went inside and tossed the sausages onto the table. She blew a stray wisp of hair out of her face and contemplated what to do next. During her earlier search for food, she'd found a frying pan and some utensils. She retrieved it, set it on the stove and, for the first time, noticed the stove was warm. Being used to such a thing back home, she'd given it no mind until now. Nate must've built a fire and banked it before he'd left the house that morning. "How considerate..." she whispered to herself. But then, maybe he'd built it for her to use to make them lunch. "What else would he build a fire for?" she asked aloud. "Of

course he built it so you could make him lunch!"
she chastised, and then noticed the coffee pot sitting
on the stove. She spied a dishrag, snatched it up,
and used it to take hold of the pot to see if he'd left
her any of the brew. She was surprised to find it was
full. Had the man made himself coffee, then a fresh
pot for her?

Guilt sank deep into the pit of her belly in that
moment. She set the coffee pot back onto the stove
with a loud clunk. She then went about cooking the
man sausages for his lunch. The thought that he'd
do such a thing for her after she'd made him sleep
on the floor last night was too much. Maybe she
should go back to Beckham. The warm bath he'd
prepared for her the night before, the coffee he'd
made her this morning, not to mention leaving her
the only biscuit left to them. Did he have one? Or
had he saved it for her?

She tried not to think about it anymore as she
placed the sausages in the hot pan and rolled them
around with a fork. She'd watched her brother,
Hank, cook sausages much the same way, and
figured if he could do it, so could she. He often
made a quick snack for Bert, Percy, and himself
when no one else was around to do it. The thought
that her brother was a better cook than she was,
rankled, but what could she do other than learn?

It wasn't long before a chill went up her spine at
the sound of loud hoof beats coming to an abrupt
stop outside the cabin. She spun to the door just as it
opened. Nate entered, stopped, and stared at her.
She swallowed hard. "Hello," she managed to
squeak out.

His eyes grew wide. "Are you… cooking?"

She turned to look at the stove. "I think so."

"You think so?" he echoed as he crossed the room to the cook stove. He peeked into the frying pan, plucked the fork from her hand, and gave the sausages a turn. "You have to keep moving them around or they burn." He eyed the stove a moment. "Not that these would; the fire is too low." He moved the pan aside and reached for the wood box near the stove. He took a few pieces, put them in, stoked the fire, and then closed the firebox again. "There, that's better." He turned and looked down at her.

Libby fought the urge to shrink under his gaze and, instead, stared boldly back. "Where have you been?"

"Riding the fence line, looking for weak spots. We'll be mending fences all afternoon, I reckon." He continued to stare at her as he took a seat. "So tell me, Mrs. Dalton. Did you sleep well last night?"

SIX

His wife blushed a furious red.

Nate placed his elbows on the table and leaned toward her. "Aren't you going to ask me how I slept?"

She swallowed hard and bit her lower lip. She was nervous, he could tell. Good. "Did you?"

"Did I what?" he taunted.

"Did you... sleep well?"

He sat back in his chair and smiled. "Why, I'm glad you asked me that. No, I did not."

She swallowed again and he could see her falter but a moment, before she squared her shoulders and looked him in the eye. "I'm sorry to hear that," she said as she plucked the fork from the table and turned to the stove. She began to push the sausages around in the frying pan. "I'm sorry you didn't sleep well," she added without looking at him.

Nate pressed his lips together. She sounded remorseful, and it pricked his pride. "I've got a mighty nice bed in there, haven't I?"

She looked over her shoulder at him. "Yes, it is nice. Wherever did you get it?"

"I ordered it from a catalog they had at the

mercantile in Weatherford. Right fancy, don't you think?"

"Very much so," she said and turned to face him. Fork still in hand, she came to the table and sat. She then stared at the tabletop, and said nothing.

"I plan on sleeping in that bed of mine tonight," he said, his voice soft. "Where are you going to sleep?"

That got her attention. Her head snapped up as her eyes went wide. "Where... do you want me to sleep?"

He leaned forward again and looked into her eyes. "As much as it pains me to say this, I forgive you. But don't ever... and I do mean *ever*... lock me out of that bedroom again, do you hear me?"

She audibly gulped before nodding, and never once took her eyes from his.

"Now," he said as he sat back in his chair again. "Here are the reasons why."

Her mouth dropped open. "What?"

"Hush up and listen," he instructed, his tone soft and even. He didn't want to frighten her, but needed to get his point across. "One," he said as he held up a finger. "It's not safe. What if something was to happen to you, and I couldn't get in? Lord, woman, I'd have to bust the window out to do it. Two," he said and held up another finger. "It's disrespectful. I wouldn't have laid a hand on you last night if you told me that's what you wanted. You didn't have to lock me out to make sure."

She paled and tears streamed down her face. At least he knew he was getting his point across.

"Three." Another finger went up. "That floor's mighty cold, and I don't relish sleeping on it again!

Check the sausages."

She scrambled up from the table and went to the stove. Libby pushed them around again. "I…" she began and turned to him, a helpless look on her face. "I think… they're done," she stammered. Then, of course, she burst into tears.

Nate put his face in his hands a moment and shook his head. What an idiot! He didn't think he was being hard on her, but apparently she hadn't developed much backbone yet. He got up from the table, stepped around it, and went to her. "Now, there's no need for all those waterworks. Give me that," he said, and snatched the fork from her hand and looked at the contents of the frying pan. Lunch was ready. "Go get a couple of plates out of the sideboard, will you?"

She gaped at him, tears streaming down her face. He didn't see it coming. She slapped him. Nate was glad the frying pan wasn't in his hand, or he might have accidentally dropped it on her foot. He stood in silence and put a hand to his cheek, the sting of her slap still evident. He studied her as she stared up at him in defiance. "What'd you do that for?" He thought giving her some boundaries would convince her he had her best interests in mind and respected her. His little Libby, however, still didn't understand.

She didn't answer him, and instead gave him her back.

"Oh, no you don't," he said as he reached out, grabbed her, and spun her to face him. He pulled her against him and locked her in his arms. "You're going to explain yourself.

"Let go of me!"

"No, not until you tell me why you just slapped my face." She began to cry again, more out of anger than anything else. A good thing; he'd hate to think he'd married a milk-sop of a woman. "Well?" he demanded.

Libby stopped her struggles and glared up at him. "You bawled me out… and then…think it's all okay?"

"Isn't it?"

She shook her head, unable to speak, as tears streamed down her face again. For the life of him, he would never understand women!

"We need to settle this, now," he said as he sat and pulled her onto his lap.

"What are you doing?" she screeched.

"Sitting; what does it look like? Now stop your squirming and listen to me."

She stopped; whether because she was tuckered out at this point, or actually minding him, he wasn't sure. He was just glad she was still. "What do you want?" she asked.

He looked her in the eye. "I want us to start being a husband and wife. Now is that too much to ask?"

She shook her head, stopped, then nodded, shook it again. "I… I…"

"You what? Lord, woman, you're not making this easy."

"But it's not easy," she said in a weak voice. "It'll never be easy."

He held her tighter, even though she wasn't struggling. She felt good in his arms and he wanted her closer. "Libby," he said, his voice tender. "We don't know each other yet; of course it's not easy.

Who said it would be?"

She looked into his eyes, as her lower lip trembled. "I'm sorry if I'm not what you expected. I'm not a good cook like Bonnie or beautiful like Gwen. I'm sorry if you're not pleased with me."

"Pleased with you? How can I be? We just got married yesterday."

"I spoiled your wedding night."

"Spoiled my… are you still on that? Look, darlin', so I slept on the floor last night. I understand you had to be scared. Heck, you hadn't even been kissed until yesterday."

She looked at him in shock. "How do you know that?"

"A man can tell."

She looked away. "Oh, I see."

He tucked a finger under her chin and pulled her face toward his. "Libby, I won't share my bed with you in that way until you're ready." His eyes locked on hers and held her just as tightly as his arms.

Her breathing picked up as her mouth hung open in shock. "You… you won't?" came out in a high pitched chirp.

"That's not how I want my marriage to start. I've had women in my life who… well, let's just say they didn't want to take the time to get to know me. But you… you I'd like to get to know first."

"You… you mean you really will woo me?"

He smiled and stroked her cheek with the back of a finger. "If wooing you, Libby Dalton, means getting to know you better, then yes, that's what I'll do."

Ever so slowly, her mouth curved up into a shy smile. She then gasped. "The sausages!" She struggled to free herself. He let her go as he realized their lunch was burning. "Oh no!" Libby cried as she looked into the pan. "I think we killed them!"

Nate laughed. "That's okay, sweetheart. We'll survive it."

Nate got up from the table and rushed to Libby's side. He took a dishrag, grabbed the smoking hot pan, and pulled it to one side of the stove. "Get us a plate," he ordered.

Libby did as he asked and went to the sideboard, got a plate, and then held it out to him. He flipped the sausages onto the plate and pointed at the table. She set the food on the table, and then fetched another fork and a knife. He motioned for her to sit, and she did. He sat in the chair next to her, and proceeded to cut the sausages into bite-sized pieces. They were terribly burnt on one side, but the rest of them looked okay. He handed her the fresh fork, then bowed his head for the blessing. "Thank you, Lord, for this food," he said. "And thank you for this new beginning, amen."

Libby looked at him. His eyes were intent on hers. "Thank you."

He stabbed a piece of sausage. "For what?"

"For understanding."

He gave her a hint of a smile. "Don't mention it. Do *you* understand all the things I told you earlier?"

"I think so," she said as she poked at a piece of meat.

"It's my job to protect you, Libby, and I'll do it

as I see fit. But when you don't talk to me, you make my job harder, do you understand?"

"Yes," she said then stabbed her fork into the sausage.

"Good," he said and took another piece. "I'm glad we've got that out of the way and understand each other."

They ate in silence until all the meat was gone. Libby felt relieved, on the one hand, but very unsure of herself on the other. What did he mean he was glad they got that out of the way? She was having a hard enough time understanding as it was! She watched as he stood up from the table. "Are you leaving now?"

"I have to be getting back to work."

Libby stood. "Oh ..."

"Do you?" he asked, his voice husky as he closed the distance between them. He rested his hands on her shoulders and looked into her eyes. "Have to get back to work, I mean."

She gazed at him a moment, then closed them. She let out a small gasp when she felt his lips touch her own in a gentle kiss. "Try not to burn supper," he said, then gently patted her cheek.

By the time Libby opened her eyes, Nate was gone. "I'll try not to," she whispered as she reached up and touched her lips with a finger. She stared at the door as a chill went up her spine. She licked her lips, wondering if she could taste his on them. When he'd kissed her the day before at their wedding, she was too shocked to notice the pleasure of it, but not this time. This time, Nate's kiss lingered and warmed her like she'd never been warmed before.

Libby stepped to the nearest chair and sat. Maybe her husband didn't think she was so bad after all. And if he didn't think so, then why should she? But before she had time to ponder the possibilities, Bonnie was knocking on her door. It was time to bake the bread.

The rest of the afternoon was spent baking bread and learning how to make stew. Libby found it hard to concentrate, and twice Bonnie scolded her for not paying attention. But all she could think of was Nate's kiss, one she'd had no idea was coming, and that somehow made it special. She didn't know why, but wished she did. Perhaps because he kissed her out of his own free will, not because she whined or manipulated him into it, or resorted to batting her eyes at him. No, he'd kissed her because he'd wanted to, and the thought made her feel pretty.

"Libby, are you all right?" Gwen asked. "You're all red!"

Bonnie studied her and smiled. "She's fine. Let's finish this stew then divide it between the three of us."

Soon it was time for Libby and Bonnie to leave and, with wrapped bread loaves in one hand, and of pot of stew held between them, they left Gwen and Walt's cabin to go home. When they got to Libby's, Bonnie took the pot of stew and put half of it into the frying pan still on the stove. Thankfully, it was getting dark, and Bonnie hadn't noticed that something had already been cooked in said frying pan. Libby wondered how the stew would taste mixed with sausage fat, and supposed in a short while she'd find out.

"There, now you have dinner for Nate. I'd better get back to the cabin and be ready with Bart's when he gets home."

"What's Bart like?" Libby asked, curious.

Bonnie stood stock still. After a moment, she finally said, "Agreeable." With that, she left.

Libby stared after her as she walked toward her own cabin at a quick pace. "Agreeable?" Libby echoed. "What does that mean?" She didn't have time to think on it further as Nate rode up. He dismounted his horse, a big bay, then smiled at her in the low light of dusk. "Evening, darlin'," he said with a grin.

"Hello," she said, a shy smile on her face.

"Do I smell something?" he asked.

Libby nodded. "Bonnie taught us how to make stew. There's some on the stove. Bread, too."

"You don't say," he said with a grin. "I'd best put Jack up, and then come in and try some."

"He's a nice horse," Libby commented as she admired his mount, and gave the horse a pat on the neck.

"Yeah, he is," Nate agreed and stroked the animal's muzzle. "Me and Jack, here, have been through a lot together, haven't we boy? He looked at her. "Can you ride?"

Libby paled and shook her head. "No, I never learned."

"Best we remedy that, eh?"

"What?!"

"You heard me. If you're going to be a rancher's wife, you'll have to learn how to ride."

"But... but..."

"No buts. First riding lesson will be Sunday,

after church."

"Church!" she croaked.

"Of course, church. Ain't you a God-fearing woman?"

"Well... I... yes... But where do we go to church?"

"In Wiggieville, about an hour from here."

Libby hadn't thought of this sort of thing yet. Her mind had been too full of their disastrous wedding night, and of today's lunch. Though, *that* hadn't been so disastrous.

"Riding lessons," she muttered as she turned to the door.

"Yep. But don't worry, I'm a good teacher."

She turned to him and tried not to grimace. "I hope I'll be as good a student."

He laughed, took Jack by the reins, and headed for the barn. Libby went inside and closed the door behind her. When she'd agreed to this marriage, no one told her horses would be involved! It was enough to learn how to bake bread that day, not to mention stew. Would Gwen and Bonnie have to learn how to ride? Libby swallowed hard. "Oh dear, how am I going to tell him that I'm terrified of horses? At least, the riding part."

SEVEN

The next several days for Libby and Gwen were spent trying to learn to be a good wife.

If they weren't at Gwen's cabin cooking, cleaning, mending, and—*shudder*—doing the laundry, they were at Libby's. Never did they do their lessons at Bonnie's house, until today.

Bonnie opened the door when Gwen knocked, and smiled at her sisters. "Good morning! Are you ready to get started?"

"As ready as we'll ever be," said Gwen as she pushed her way inside. Libby had the good sense to wait a moment, though she was just as curious to see Bart and Bonnie's place. Before she had a chance to look, Gwen stopped up short and gasped. Libby hurried inside at the sound, ran into her, and nearly knocked both of them over.

Bonnie shut the door a little harder than she should, causing her sisters to jump. "I know it's not much," she said evenly. "Bart doesn't like a lot of clutter."

"Clutter?" Gwen huffed. "What clutter?"

"Exactly," said Bonnie.

Libby glanced at the sparse furnishings—crude

at best—and the lack of feminine touches. Of course, without the proper supplies to make things such as curtains or tablecloths, how could there be? There was a single chair, a small table, and a crate. A far cry from Libby's cabin, or even Gwen's. "I had no idea…" Libby whispered.

"Neither did I," Bonnie muttered under her breath as she walked past her sisters and headed for the cook stove. "I thought we'd try our hand at baking cakes today. Men love cake."

Gwen was still gawking at the bare walls, floor, and, well… *everything.* "How can you stand it?"

"I've grown accustomed."

Libby felt a pang of guilt. Her cabin was lovely, incredible, and that was compared to Gwen's, which was much more… *practical.* As far as Walton was concerned, he saw no reason to change it. Gwen, of course, had already done a few things to make it more her own, whereas Libby didn't have to do a thing. To her, Nate had done a beautiful job furnishing and decorating his little place. But this… was downright dismal. No wonder Bonnie hadn't had them over until now.

"Bonnie, I won't stand for it," Gwen said, her voice stern.

"Stand for what?"

"This!" she said as she waved her arms to indicate the room. "It's awful!"

"Gwen! Don't tell her that!" Libby scolded.

"It's all right, Libby," said Bonnie. "Besides, you know Gwenny's not one to keep her opinion to herself. And she's right, it is awful. But I can live with it."

"You shouldn't have to," Libby told her. "After

all you've done to help us, maybe we can help you."

"Yes!" Gwen chimed in. "If you teach us how to sew, we could make a tablecloth, curtains, all kinds of things for you!"

Bonnie's mouth dropped half-open as she stared at her sisters in shock. "Really?"

"Of course," said Libby. "Gwen's right; after all you've done for us, we should do something for you. Of course, she's also right about the fact that you'll have to teach us how to sew to enable us to do so."

Bonnie's eyes darted between the two of them a few times, before she burst out laughing. Gwen and Libby exchanged a quick look, and joined her. It took a few moments for the three women to calm down before one of them got enough air in their lungs to speak. "Let's get started on these cakes, ladies," Bonnie sputtered. "And then we'll see about a sewing lesson."

"How are we going to sew anything?" asked Gwen. "Do you have a needle and thread? Walton had a little, but not much. Does Bart?"

Bonnie quickly calmed and glanced around the cabin. "You know, you're right. I've used up what thread I could find to mend some of Bart's things. We're going to need supplies if we're to make anything for this place. I'll see about a trip to town. In the meantime, let's bake."

They made several cakes that afternoon. The first was a disaster, even with Bonnie telling Gwen and Libby what to do. The next two fared better, and Bonnie told them that by next week they would be making their own. Libby prayed she wouldn't destroy hers. Gwen bypassed any prayers and announced, "Mine's going to die. I already know I'll never be able to do this!" But, after a few reassuring words from Bonnie, Gwen's attitude toward her baking skills improved. Soon it was time to go home and prepare supper for their husbands.

"What are you going to try not to burn tonight?" Libby asked Gwen as they strolled back the their cabins, each carrying a cake.

"I haven't decided yet. You?"

"A couple of nights ago I murdered some eggs for Nate. I think I'll try another stab at it."

"You're going to stab your eggs to murder them this time?" teased Gwen.

Libby rolled her eyes. "You know what I mean. I thought maybe I could fry some eggs and put them on bread for sandwiches."

That's a good idea. Walt liked it when I made him some. Maybe I'll make him egg sandwiches again tonight."

"You've already made them that way?"

"Yes. You mean I've done something you haven't?"

Libby sighed. "You've probably done a lot that I haven't."

Gwen studied her. "Don't worry, you'll catch up."

Libby looked at her and smiled. "I hope so."

When they got to Libby's, they hugged each other as best they could (no mean feat when each of them held a cake in her hands), and agreed to let the other know how the eggs went the next day. Unfortunately, the next day was Sunday. Libby's heart pounded in her chest as Gwen walked away. How was she going to get out of the riding lesson

Nate wanted to give her? She still hadn't gotten up the courage to tell him about her fear of horses. Well, not the horses themselves, but the riding part. And then it hit her. "Of course! That's what I'll do!" She smiled as she sighed in relief, and went inside to fix her husband his supper.

Nate and his brothers parted ways at their usual spot and headed to their individual cabins. He wondered if Walton or Bart noticed he'd been out of sorts the past couple of days, and were just being quiet about it. Yesterday, Walt, a huge smile on his face, boldly asked him how Libby was in bed. The question took Nate by surprise at first, but then he took in his brother's bright eyes and wide smile, and knew what his own situation must be. Nate returned his smile and simply said, "warm." Which, of course, she was. When he got the chance to hold her, that is.

They shared the bed at night, but not each other. He didn't know how much longer he could hold out. Even in a nightdress, her body completely covered, he could not only see her curves, but swore he could *feel* them, and without laying a hand on her to boot! He didn't know how such a thing could happen, but it did. He *knew* what she would feel like before he touched her. When he did have the chance—as twice she snuggled against him in the middle of the night—he reveled in the feel of her as she tucked her body up to his. For some reason, it brought out every protective instinct he had, and it was all he could do to release her in the morning before she woke.

By the third night, he vowed to make her love him. So what if she was ill-fitted for ranch life; that was now. He'd teach her, by the grace of God he would! He'd teach her to ride, shoot, hunt, and work the land! Or, in this case, a vegetable garden. But, he'd still teach her how to herd cows, just in case.

When he got home, he took care of Jack, finished up a few more chores in the barn, and then went inside. When he entered the cabin, Libby was slicing bread. "Hello, darlin'," he greeted with a smile. "What did your sister teach you today?"

She pointed to a pile of... *something*... on a plate sitting atop the sideboard. "Dessert!" she said proudly.

Nate stared at *it* from where he stood, took off his coat and hat, and hung them on a peg near the door. "What *is* that?"

"A cake, of course. Or supposed to be. At least I didn't burn it." She said it with such innocence, it almost hurt. But then, that's what he loved about her. She was pure, and of course, naïve. But she could be taught things, and when she learned how to survive, he'd have himself a wife.

Of course, if she were able to cook someday, that would help. "Does it taste good?"

"The one we tested did... sort of," she said with a grin.

He returned her smile. Her confidence was growing, and made her very attractive, not that she wasn't pretty to begin with, but a woman who believed in herself was someone a man could count on. If his guess was right, his little Libby didn't know who she was yet. Bart's wife, Bonnie, knew her own mettle which, in Nate's opinion, made Bart the luckiest of the three. He wouldn't have to help his wife along and teach her to live as a rancher's wife. Walt, too, was lucky, in the fact that his wife, though as unskilled in her domestic abilities as Libby, was obviously not opposed to learning a thing or two in the bedroom. Nate's wife, on the other hand, was under-skilled in both areas. *For now.*

Nate smiled at the thought and went to sit at the kitchen table. "What's for supper?"

"Er... well," she began, her tone sheepish. "As we spent so much time baking this afternoon, I thought we could just have fried egg sandwiches."

"Egg sandwiches?" he repeated thoughtfully. "As hungry as I am, I could eat three, if you can manage it."

She stared at him a moment before she smoothed the skirt of her dress. He noticed she did it when she was nervous. "I have a goal tonight," she announced. "Since I didn't burn the cake, and only had a little trouble getting it out of the pan, I'll try to do the same with the eggs."

He tried not to laugh, but a chuckle escaped, nonetheless. "All right; can I watch?"

"Oh, must you?"

"Would it make things harder if I do?"

"A little," she said as she blushed.

Nate smiled again, his eyes darting to her mouth. She was so adorable, he almost couldn't stand it. He wanted to take her in his arms, kiss her senseless, then carry her to the bedroom.

Patience, Nate old boy, patience ... his good

sense warned. He took a deep breath and glanced at the hearth. "It's a little chilly in here," he remarked. "I think I'll build us a fire."

Her eyes lit up. "Oh, would you? I'd love to have a fire."

Nate hadn't use the fireplace for a while. The stove was enough to keep the cabin warm at this time of year. "Very well; while you make supper, I'll take care of keeping you... uh... cozy."

She blushed again. The sight of her pink cheeks made him stop and stare. Time to take a chance and see how ready she was.

He went around the table to stand in front of her, reached up, and brushed a stray lock of hair out of her face. "Did you know you're mighty pretty when you're cooking?"

Her blush deepened. "You mean, when I'm *trying* to?"

"Trying or succeeding, darlin', it doesn't matter. You're still pretty when you're doing it." He bent to her and gave her a gentle kiss on the cheek, straightened, and winked. He then went to the hearth to get a fire going.

He sensed her watching him. He hadn't kissed her since the day they'd had their little "talk". And though it had been a few days, she'd been too quiet for his taste. Like a frightened filly, she would take some extra time and effort, but he knew once she started to trust him, and understood he wasn't going to hurt her, she'd start to open up and let her walls down. Maybe then, he could do the same. Lord knew he'd had them up for far too long. He couldn't afford to fall in love these past years, as he didn't know where he'd end up. Nate always sensed that somehow, someway, he'd settle near his brothers. He just didn't know when. He'd forgotten the notion until he received Walt's letter, asking him to come to Texas and start ranching. Reading that letter the same day he got a good knock on the head with a piece of firewood, brought it to mind. Now here he was, settled near his brothers, with what promised to be one of the biggest ranches in this part of Texas. He even had a wife, thanks to Walton's ingenuity. Now all he had to do was break her in. But this wasn't some horse he was going to train, but a woman. She just didn't know how to be one yet.

Nate smiled. One thing was for certain. He was going to enjoy teaching her.

Libby watched Nate eat his sandwiches from across the table. How could the sight of a man eating warm her so? Maybe it was the fact he enjoyed the meal, or that she hadn't

ruined supper for once. Whatever it was, she hoped the warm flutter in her belly and the delicious chills that went up her spine lasted the rest of the evening. They made her want to snuggle against him on the settee and gaze at the fire. Of course, her disaster of a cake might ruin the mood. That is, if it didn't taste good. With luck, it only *looked* awful.

Nate sat back in his chair and patted his stomach. "That was some mighty fine eatin', darlin'. Thank you."

Libby blushed at his praise. "You're welcome."

"Need some help with the dishes?"

Libby started in her chair. He'd never offered to help her with the dishes before. "If you like."

"Sure, why not?" he said as he stood. She watched him disappear for a moment as he went out back to fetch some water, brought it into the kitchen, and then put it on the stove to heat. He then put on a pot of coffee to have with their dessert.

"Did I do something wrong?" Libby asked. Why else would he be taking over what she'd come to learn were *her* chores?

"No, not at all."

"Then why are you doing everything?"

He glanced around the kitchen before his eyes settled on her. "Can't a man spend time with his wife? I'd rather be doing something with you than just sitting at the table, watching you."

Libby could only stare. Her father never helped her mother. Come to think of it, her parents hadn't done much of anything together. The thought that Nate wanted to be at her side made the flutters in her stomach turn into summersaults. She smiled at him. "We could have our cake and coffee while the water's heating."

"That's the idea, darlin'," he said with a wink.

Another chill went up her spine and her shoulders shook with the force of it.

"Is something wrong?" he asked as he stepped to her.

She gazed up at him, adoration in her eyes. He was being so thoughtful and patient, she felt weak in the knees. "Nothing," she breathed.

He took a step closer and put a warm hand on her shoulder. "You wouldn't be lying to me now, would you?" he asked in a soft voice.

Libby melted on the spot. Her knees almost buckled. "Uh-uh," she said with a shake of her head as she looked up at him dreamily.

Nate grinned. "That's good to know, Mrs. Dalton. Let's have some cake."

He turned and went to the sideboard. Libby's body followed of its own accord, and before she knew it, she was right behind him. He turned around and almost dropped the plate. "Whoa," he drawled. "Where'd you come from?"

Libby looked over her shoulder to where she'd been standing, and pointed.

Nate laughed, and she delighted in the way his shoulders shook with his mirth. "Let's sit down and try this concoction of yours."

"I'll check the coffee," she squeaked as she gathered her senses. What was *wrong* with her? Good heavens! She'd followed him to the sideboard like some love-sick puppy! She spun on her heel and went to the stove. "I don't think it's ready yet."

"It's not; give it a few more minutes. In the meantime, come here."

She glanced at him. He was already sitting at the table. He smiled again and patted his knee. Libby's eyes widened. Did he want her to sit on his lap? She approached him slowly, cautiously, as she caught the gleam in his eyes. What did it mean? When she reached him, he snaked an arm out, wrapped it around her waist, and pulled her onto his lap. "There now, isn't this cozy?"

She looked at him, not knowing what to do. "Is it?"

"I don't know, let's find out," he said in a rush.

Then, he tickled her.

Libby let out a shriek. His hands and fingers were everywhere! Within seconds, he had her pinned against him with one arm, as his other went from one end of her body to the next, and tickled her without mercy. She screamed for him to stop, but to no avail. After a few more moments of the delightful torture, he did. "Do you think the coffee is ready yet?"

Libby gasped for breath, unable to talk.

"Guess not!" he chortled, and started in again.

"Don't! Please!" she managed through her raucous giggles.

Nate heeded her plea and stopped again. "Why, Mrs. Dalton, I do believe you're ticklish."

Before she realized what she was doing, her arms went around his neck, her face inches from his own. "Terribly so!"

He laughed, as she continued to giggle. But when his lips touched hers, her giggles came to an end, and were replaced by a soft moan. This time, his kiss was not an introduction to his mouth, but a proclamation of what, and who, he was as a man. Libby was shocked when her arms tightened around his neck and he put a hand in her hair in response, anchoring her in place. He deepened the kiss, and somewhere in the back of her mind she wondered if she'd be able to breathe. Yet at the same time, Libby also found she didn't care.

EIGHT

By the time Sunday rolled around, Libby had her plan in place. It was simple, really. She'd invite her sisters and their husbands to lunch after church. If she kept them there long enough, there'd be no time for Nate to give her a riding lesson! Especially if she and Gwen were going to cook! As soon as Nate hitched up their wagon, she put her plan into action.

Libby nonchalantly pulled on her gloves as Nate entered the cabin. "Are you ready to go?" he asked.

"Yes," she said. "I… I was wondering…"

He looked down at her and smiled. "Hmm?"

She couldn't help but smile back. For several nights now, they'd shared the same bed. The last two she'd woken up in his arms. "Could we invite your brothers and my sisters over after church for lunch?"

Nate took a deep breath and thought a moment. "I don't see why not."

Libby smiled at him again and took a step closer. He closed the remaining distance between them and wrapped his arm around her. "I was kind of hoping to have you to myself today, as it's our first Sunday together."

"Oh," she said as her breath hitched. "That's true, isn't it? But I thought it would be nice for everyone if we got together today."

"Very well, we'll have them over."

Libby sent him a brilliant smile. "Thank you."

"Let's go," he told her. "We don't want to be late."

Libby took a deep breath. Now that she'd be spared the riding lesson that afternoon, she relaxed. But she still needed to make it through the morning services. What was church going to be like? It would be the first time she and her sisters would meet the townsfolk of Wiggieville. What were they going to think of the Dalton men sending off for mail-order brides? She'd always thought of it as being a last resort, on both ends! For Libby and her sisters, it was a form of escape. But what about Walt, Nate, and Bart Dalton? Had they done it out of desperation? Or practicality? Maybe there weren't any single women in Wiggieville.

When they reached the church and entered, Libby's eyes grew wide. The church was full. She didn't expect to see so many people, most of whom were men. Several sidled up to Gwen as soon as Walt wandered off to speak with some of the other townsfolk. One man in particular seemed overly interested, and Libby's hackles went up.

"I'm John Jenkins."

Gwen smiled and held her hand out for him to shake. "I'm Gwen Blue. I mean, Gwen Dalton."

Libby fought the urge to roll her eyes. Surely Gwen wouldn't start flirting with the man?

John took her hand and brought it to his lips. "It will be so nice to have a beautiful lady to look at on Sunday mornings."

Libby stiffened at his action. How dare he! Her head snapped to Gwen just as she snatched her hand away. Bonnie must have seen him do it, as she was suddenly on the other side of their sister. They now flanked her as Mr. Jenkins gave Gwen an oily smile.

Gwen shook her head. "I'm a married woman, Mr. Jenkins."

Libby's eyes widened in surprise. Gwen *wasn't* going to flirt with him?

He shrugged. "Men die young out here. Just staking my claim." He tipped his hat at the three ladies and wandered off.

Libby glared at Gwen nonetheless. "You can't encourage the men here, Gwenny. None of us need the kind of scandal we had at home!"

"I didn't encourage him, Libby. He walked up to me and introduced himself, and the next thing I knew he was kissing my hand. I certainly didn't *ask* him to!"

Libby looked skeptical even as Bonnie patted Gwen's arm. "I'm sorry. It was unfair of us to assume you'd done something wrong without knowing all the facts."

Gwen gave her sister a brief nod, and wandered across the church to where Walt stood talking to the preacher.

Libby let out a long sigh then shrugged when she noticed Bonnie eyeing her. "She's learning, just like the rest of us. Don't be so quick to think Gwenny can't change."

Libby cringed at the scolding as Bonnie turned to find Bart. She tried to shake off her sister's words as she went to look for Nate. Bonnie was right, of course. When wasn't she? With another sigh, Libby found Nate and together they took a seat.

The service wasn't overly long, and Libby found it a pleasant diversion. She still had to make sure her sisters and their husbands had lunch with them. As soon as the service was over, she made a beeline for the nearest sister. "Bonnie, would you and Bart like to have lunch with Nate and me? I'm going to invite Gwen and Walt as well."

"I suppose we could. What are you making?"

Whatever will take an enormous amount of time, she thought, but said, "Err... I have no idea."

"I do; I have something already prepared. I can bring it over."

Libby paled. *Oh no!* "Ah, but wouldn't it be nice if Gwen and I tried to make something for everyone?"

"Everyone?" Bonnie repeated. Libby studied her. Was she turning pale?

"Of course," said Libby. "You have to admit, we do need to practice."

"Yes, exactly," said Bonnie with a grimace.

"I'll go invite Gwen!" offered Libby.

"And I'll tell Bart, but *I'm* bringing lunch. I've made a stew and have fresh biscuits."

Now Libby paled. What was she going to do? If Bonnie brought lunch, they'd only be together for an hour or so! Then Nate would want to give her a riding lesson! What to do? She tried to think as she sought Gwen, found her, and offered the invitation. Gwen, of course, asked the obvious. "Who's doing the cooking?"

Libby tried not to grimace. "Bonnie is making lunch. But I have the best table for entertaining. We thought it would be nice to have all six of us sit down for lunch together." Naturally, she knew what Gwen's answer would be. Anytime Gwen saw a chance not to cook, she took it.

However, Gwen did offer to bring something, which made Libby smile. Bonnie suggested she bring jam for the biscuits, and Gwen was happy to comply.

When they returned to the ranch, Libby tried not to let Nate see how nervous she was. She hurried into the cabin, determined to make lunch last as long as possible. Before she knew it, Bonnie and Bart were knocking on their door. They'd brought the stew and biscuits. Bart hauled the pot to the stove and set it down as Bonnie put a pan of biscuits in the warming oven. "Where's Nate," he asked.

"In the barn," said Libby.

Bart tipped his hat and left the cabin to seek out his brother. Bonnie took the lid off the stew and gave it a stir. Libby plopped into the nearest chair and tried not to look anxious. No sooner had she sat than Gwen walked into the cabin. She proudly set a jar of jam on the table and looked at Bonnie. "Do you need any help?"

Bonnie shook her head and suggested that they set the table. Libby's mind was still racing as she and Gwen did as she asked. She went to the sideboard in a rush. She was more nervous about this riding lesson than she thought. *Slow down, Libby, will you?* she thought to herself. *Even if you do have to get on a horse, Nate will be right there!*

He's not going to let me fall... Is he?

Libby took out a fresh tablecloth and napkins, along with the dishes and silverware they would need. Within moments, she and Gwen had the table looking as nice as the one at home in Beckham. A wave of homesickness hit out of the blue, and Libby almost stumbled. She missed her brothers, her mother; she even missed Pa. But that didn't mean she still wasn't angry with him. She pushed thoughts of home aside, took a step back and eyed the table. "It needs something, doesn't it?"

Gwen could only shrug in response. Making *herself* look beautiful was her greatest talent. Anything *else;* not so much. Libby tried not to sigh at the thought when the men came into the cabin. They wiped their feet, hung their hats, and crossed the room to the table. Nate had a funny look on his face, and Libby wondered what he was up to. "For my beautiful wife," he said with a smile, and produced a small bouquet of flowers he had hidden behind his back.

Libby gasped in delight, despite the fact she was so nervous. "That's just what we needed!" Seeking another distraction, she fetched the one vase in the house, went out back to the pump, and filled it with water. She then returned to the kitchen and arranged the flowers in the vase. Setting it on the table, she admired her handiwork. "Isn't that better, Gwen?"

Gwen gave her a blank look and nodded. "Table's set, Bonnie. Anything else we can do?"

Bonnie told her to pour everyone a cup of coffee. She did, and soon they were all seated and ready to eat. Before Nate so much as opened his mouth, Walt said the blessing.

Their meal had begun.

Libby wondered if it would be her last. What if she fell off the horse and broke her neck? It would serve Nate right for wanting to teach her how to ride! Libby had to force herself to calm down. Otherwise, the others might notice her hands were shaking. *For Heaven's sakes Libby!* she thought. *Get a hold of yourself!* Her eyes darted around the table, and she hoped no one noticed how she'd begun to fidget. It was then that *she* noticed how happy everyone looked. Well, fairly happy. Walton Dalton, of course, topped the list. He looked downright ecstatic!

The three couples talked about this and that, until it was all Libby could do not to choke on her food. Her nerves were getting more frazzled by the minute. One would think she was going to be taken out to hang. Is this how one felt when walking to the gallows? Had someone just asked her a question? Good grief! She didn't even know who was talking to her! How much more nervous could she be? Maybe she'd better pay attention to the conversation. But by the time she did, the meal ended. Her time of reckoning had come.

Bonnie and Gwen helped Libby do the dishes, and clean up the kitchen as the men went into the living room and talked. Soon, after everyone left, the cabin was quiet but for the audible gulp that escaped her.

"Something the matter?" asked Nate, concerned.

She shook her head. She was so scared at this point she couldn't speak!

Nate went to where she stood by the stove. "Libby? Are you all right?"

Should she say she was? Pretend she was sick? Die on the spot? Okay, so maybe that was a bit drastic...

"Libby, darlin', what's wrong?"

"No ... no ... nothing," she stammered. "Everything's fine."

"Good, you wait right here. I'm gonna go saddle Jack."

"What?" she squeaked. Her knees went weak and she had to grip the nearest chair for support.

Nate didn't notice as he headed for the door, whistling, no less! Did he have to be so happy about her upcoming demise? "I'll be right back," he called over his shoulder.

Libby fell onto the chair with the weight of a boulder on her. Maybe if she were one, Nate wouldn't be able to lift her into the saddle! She rapidly wiped her hands on the skirt of her dress, unable to think. What was she going to do? What if she landed on her head? Broke an arm? A leg? Maybe if she paid attention as she fell off, she could land on Nate!

"Ready?"

Libby yelped in surprise, and jumped from the chair. She hadn't even heard him come in!

"What is *wrong* with you?" Nate demanded.

"Uh... nothing," she said as her jaw shook. Bile rose, and she felt as if she might vomit.

Nate went to her, took a chair and sat. "There's something wrong. Tell me what it is."

She bit her lip and shook her head.

"Libby…" he warned. "What did we talk about the other day?"

She sucked in a breath and prayed she wouldn't throw up. "I… I…"

He let out a heavy sigh, and she wondered if he was impatient at this point. She then looked into his eyes. There was a tenderness held in them, and she knew instinctively it was meant for her. Her trembling lessened.

He scooted his chair closer and put his hands on her shoulders. "You're shaking like a leaf!" He looked her over a second time. "Hey now, darlin'. What's got you so riled up?"

Libby closed her eyes and shook her head. She was ashamed to tell him she couldn't ride. Worse, she was ashamed to tell him she was terrified to the point she might faint. With her luck, it wouldn't happen until she was on the horse.

Nate cupped her face with a hand and drew closer. "You can tell me. In fact, I want you to be able to tell me anything and everything that's in that head and heart of yours."

Libby relaxed another notch. "Really? You won't laugh?"

"Why would I?"

"It's silly, and stupid, and I don't have any control over it!"

"Control over what?"

"Fear," she said. The word felt as heavy as she did a few moments ago when she sat in the chair.

He studied her for a moment or two, scooted his chair even closer, and wrapped his arms around her. "What are you afraid of, darlin'?"

Libby couldn't help it. She started to cry. "Everything!"

His arms tightened around her and Libby couldn't help but relax against him. "Tell me," he said.

He hadn't laughed at her! Didn't berate her! Instead he wanted to *know*? "I'm sorry," she began. "I should have told you before."

"Told me what?"

She pulled away, looked him in the eye, and blurted, "I'm afraid of horses!"

She watched his jaw tighten and braced herself. Would he be angry?

"What happened?"

Libby started at the question and stared at him.

"Libby, why are you afraid of horses? People usually don't have this kind of fear, unless something happened to them."

"I don't know if anything happened. I've never ridden a horse before."

Nate cocked his head to one side as his brow puckered. "Well, I suppose some folks could be afraid of something they have no knowledge about. Do you think that's it?"

There it was again. Understanding. He wasn't angry with her, as she thought he would be. Instead, he was genuinely interested in the reason her fear plagued her. "I don't know. I've just always been terrified of them."

Nate loosened his hold on her and sat back in his chair. "Well then, it's time we fixed that." Without warning, he stood and pulled her up with him. "Come with me; there's someone I'd like you to meet."

Before she could protest, he dragged her out of the cabin to where he'd tethered Jake. The big bay was saddled and ready to go. Libby shook her head and dug her heels into the dirt. "Oh, Nate, please no!"

Nate turned to her and took her other hand in his. "You're not getting on him."

"I'm not?" Libby asked in shock.

"No. I just want you to meet him; get to know him a little, and he you. I think you'll find that Jack's not such a bad fella." He let go of her one hand and, still holding the other, led her to Jack. The big bay eyed them both as he swished his tail at a fly.

To Libby, the horse was huge. In fact, he was the biggest she'd ever seen or been this close to. She tightened her grip on Nate's hand. He gave hers a reassuring squeeze in response. "Jack," he said. "I'd like you to meet someone. This beautiful creature standing before you is Mrs. Libby Dalton, my wife."

NINE

The next day, Libby had a sense of freedom she had never experienced before. Her new husband had banished her fears as easily as falling off a log, and she marveled at such a talent. He'd spent the rest of the afternoon teaching her about horses; their confirmation, the different breeds, even how they thought! The man should breed and train equine, not herd cows for a living. But Nate had no desire to raise horses as yet. He was too wrapped up in helping his brothers build their ranching empire. An empire Walt was down right adamant about bringing to fruition.

After her lesson on everything to know about horses, Nate showed her how to remove Jack's tack, and then showed her how to groom him. She even brushed the beast, and was shocked when the horse gave no protest. In fact, he seemed to enjoy it.

Nate then showed her what to feed Jack, and by the time they were done, she had a sense of accomplishment. She didn't even flinch when Nate announced that he'd be giving her another lesson tomorrow.

Today she'd looked forward to not so much the

lesson itself, but spending time with her husband. It was fine to fix him breakfast, watch him eat, leave, come home, eat some more, and go to bed. But there wasn't a lot of time for interaction. Often, he was too tuckered out, and wanted to turn in after dinner. She, of course, went with him, and once under the covers, he'd pull her into his arms and held her. Last night he'd even kissed her a little before he cradled her in the crook of his arm, and stroked her hair until she fell asleep. She closed her eyes at the memory and sighed. When she thought about the things he'd done for her the last few days, she grew warm all over, and a peace settled in her heart. Was this what marriage was all about? Was this ... *Love?*

Libby sat at the table and glanced around her cheery cabin. "Oh, good heavens! Am I falling in love?"

How would she know? She'd never been in love before, and had no clue as to what it should feel like. A better question was, how to find out.

"Bonnie!"

Yes, of course, she'd ask Bonnie! When she could get her alone, that is. She didn't want to talk about this and in front of Gwen. She might make fun of her. That made Libby think.

Was Gwen already in love with Walt, and he with her? Gwen still looked annoyed at times. Bonnie, on the other hand, always looked happy with Bart. She must be in love!

Libby decided that if she didn't get a chance to ask Bonnie about it today, she'd catch her tomorrow. This particular day was going to be a busy one, and she wasn't going to waste it. Her mood was too bright and happy! It was a perfect day to go into Wiggieville and shop!

After breakfast, she and her sisters, with the help of Bart, loaded themselves into his wagon and they were off! She sensed a slight discord between Bonnie and Bart, as her sister fussed over the three of them not being able to drive to town themselves. Bart explained it was for their protection, and Libby immediately pictured Mr. Jenkins trying to flirt with Gwen in church the day before. She didn't realize till then that there was more than one Mr. Jenkins in town. In fact, there were probably quite a few. Libby was suddenly glad for Bart's company, even if Gwen and Bonnie argued the point. It was one less thing to worry about, not to mention one less thing to dampen her spirits! She chatted and giggled with Gwen, or rather at Gwen, the entire ride to town.

When they reached Wiggieville, Bart parked the wagon in front of the mercantile, then helped them out of the wagon. Well, he helped Libby and Gwen. Bonnie all but tripped out and, as luck would have it, landed in her husband's arms. Libby gawked at the feat before heading up the mercantile steps.

Bonnie's husband didn't want much to do with their shopping time, and so wandered elsewhere to wait until they were done. Nate had left some money for Libby to get what she needed, and she was excited to look at bolts of fabric. She wanted to sew a dress in the worst way. Not because she wanted one, but because she wanted to look nice for Nate. The mere thought made her blush as they entered the mercantile.

The mercantile was small, much smaller than

their father's store in Beckham. But beggars couldn't be choosers, and at least it had what they needed most; bolts of fabric, a butter churn, sewing supplies, even knitting needles and yarn. Libby and her sisters quickly got to work, each gathering the things on their lists, and it wasn't long before she and Bonnie, at least, had a pile stacked atop the mercantile counter. Gwen was still hovering over the bolts of fabric, and after settling on one, finally joined them. Libby tried not to smile. It was a bolt of corn flower-blue cloth.

While they waited for the their purchases to be wrapped up, Bonnie asked Gwen about getting a few things for Thanksgiving, even though it was a month away.

"Are we going to eat at Libby's?" Gwen asked.

The question made Libby blush with pride. She did have the nicest table, even if the others might have to bring extra dishes.

"She does have the best place for entertaining," agreed Bonnie, who then went on to talk about kitchen gardens; one more thing to add to their ever-growing list of duties. But at this point, Libby began to see how those duties helped them survive. Their husbands worked hard, very hard, and needed the care of their wives when they got home. How did they ever survive on their own before Libby and her sisters arrived? What did they eat? How did they sleep? Libby couldn't imagine sleeping alone ever again. Nate's arms were safe and strong, and she'd never slept better in her life than she had the last few nights.

As Bonnie went to fetch Bart to help them take things out to the wagon, Gwen took the opportunity to mail a letter to their Aunt Edna. They then got on the subject of laundry, of all things. Probably because neither one of them enjoyed it.

Gwen, least of all. "I don't even want to think about washing the yellow dress I came here in. It's rank."

"I don't think there's anyway we'll be able to convince Bonnie to do it for us," Libby said as she scrunched up her face. She was teasing but, at the same time, there was some truth to it. For years, they'd both depended on Bonnie to help them.

"I know. I wish we were rich, and we could just hire someone to do everything," Gwen said with the same look. "Not that I'm not happy with Walton."

"I understand exactly what you mean," Libby said with a nod. "Walt seems like a good man."

Gwen nodded. "Oh, he is. He's just...larger than life sometimes. I really think he thinks everyone should be able to do everything he can, plus a million other things. I'd like to see something he's not good at just once, you know? He even cooks better than I do."

As much as Libby would like to think otherwise, Gwen was right. Walton Dalton was larger than life, and Libby didn't envy her sister living with such a whirlwind. She did, however, believe that he was a much better cook than her sister. "Gwen, honey? The horses cook better than you do. You need to start applying yourself when Bonnie teaches us."

"There's no need to be rude, Libby."

"Sometimes there is," Libby said. She wasn't trying to be rude; she just wanted to get her point across. The Dalton men deserved to each have a good wife. The sooner Gwen learned that, the better. "Sometimes you need to hear that you can't be a spoiled brat here.

We're all going to need to work hard if we're going to make the empire Walt has in his head a reality. You say all the right things, but you don't really try while Bonnie is teaching us. You're so convinced you can't do it that you just don't."

Gwen frowned, and Libby hoped she didn't go into a tirade. Thankfully, she didn't. "That's not true. I try really hard."

"Sometimes you're your own worst enemy," Libby sighed. "Being pretty doesn't get the food cooked or the laundry done. Bonnie's willing to teach us, but she's not going to spend all her time teaching us forever, you know." She wanted to say more, but Bonnie entered the mercantile. It was time to go home.

Not long after Bart and Bonnie dropped Libby off at home, Nate showed up for lunch. "Hello, darlin'; how was your trip to town?"

Libby spun to him. "I didn't think I'd see you until supper time." Not that she minded seeing him now…

"Got done earlier than expected, and thought I'd come home and spend time with my pretty little wife." He walked to where she stood. "How are you, wife?"

Libby smiled as a chill went up her spine. She gazed up into his eyes, with a strong urge to kiss him. "Fine. And you?" her voice came out a soft lilt, and she wondered if it had anything to do with the wild flutter in her belly.

"I ain't feelin' too bad," he drawled.

"I'm afraid I don't have anything ready for you. I just got here myself."

Nate's eyes raked over her, and she noted they'd changed color. Deeper, darker ... Now what would cause that? "Maybe we can come up with something together," he said, his voice low and husky.

Libby's inside's turned to mush as her back tingled. "Maybe…"

He pulled her into his arms, gazed into her eyes, and then cupped her face with a hand. Without a word, he lowered his face and kissed her. She didn't protest in the slightest; she'd been waiting for it—*no*—make that *praying* for him to do so. His kiss was just as she imagined it would be. Powerful, filling, and if she wasn't careful, he'd have her begging for more. But then, what would be wrong with that?

Nate gently broke the kiss, and rubbed a thumb across her cheek. "I think you're beautiful, Libby. He then pulled her into his arms and held her. "My little Libby, so frightened and alone." He pulled away so he could gaze at her. "Was that just yesterday?"

She nodded, embarrassed, but didn't mind. She had acted like a frightened child the day before, and didn't want to ever be like that again. She wanted to be a woman for her husband, not some silly girl. "Are you going to teach me more about horses today?"

"You know I am," he said. "In fact, let's have a

little lesson right now. Jack's out front."

"You don't want me to ride him, do you?" she asked with a hint of panic.

"Yes and no. I'll let you sit on him, and then I'll lead him. How does that sound?"

Libby felt the familiar fear rise, but quickly batted it down. She wouldn't have to ride the horse by herself, not while Nate was in control. "All right," she said with a nod.

"Great, let's go." They went outside and, sure enough, there was Jack. He looked like he'd been napping. "Come over here, darlin', and I'll give you a leg up."

"Leg up?"

"Yeah, I'll help you mount." He showed her the stirrup, explained its use, and as he had the day before, eased her fear before he helped her climb onto the big brute.

Much to Libby's dismay, she felt dizzy atop the bay, and grabbed the saddle horn to help keep her balance. "Oh, dear…"

"It's all right," Nate soothed. "Just get your seat. He's not going anywhere. I haven't untied him yet."

Libby looked down, way down (at least to her), and saw that it was true. Jack was still tethered to the hitching post. She sighed in relief and relaxed a little. How on earth did Nate gallop across the prairie on this thing?

Nate removed the reins from the hitching post, and then glanced up at her with a wry smile. "Ready?"

"What… what are you going to do?" she asked, nervous.

"Just lead him around a little. Don't worry. It'll

be fun."

"For you, maybe," she said as she gripped the saddle horn.

Nate laughed and took a few steps forward. Jack automatically followed. Libby gripped the saddle horn harder and hung on for dear life. And to think the horse was only walking! But the feel of his huge body underneath her was foreign, as was sitting in the saddle, and she wished Nate had given her another minute to adjust. But, he was the horseman of the two, and so he must know what he was doing.

"Now, this ain't so bad, is it?" he asked as he walked beside Jack. Was he even holding onto the reins?

Libby couldn't tell from her vantage point. But she did notice she could see a lot better from her perch, and studied her surroundings. "No, not too bad," she said with a small smile. And it wasn't. In fact, the more they walked along, the more she began to enjoy the ride. There was a rhythm to Jack's movements, and she tried to relax and move with the animal.

"Ready to go faster?" Nate's asked.

"No!"

"C'mon, Libby. I think you can handle it." Before she could protest, Nate quickened his pace, as did Jack.

Libby stiffened at first then relaxed. The horse was walking faster, but that's all. She chided herself for being afraid, and figured if she would just stop worrying so much about falling off, she could enjoy herself. She *was* getting to spend time with Nate, after all.

"A little faster?"

Libby gripped the saddle horn again and braced herself. "Okay."

Nate turned to look up at her, and gave her a huge grin. "Okay, you're the boss." He then broke into a jog, as did Jack.

Libby held on tight as she was bounced along. "Pl…ease…don't ma…ma…make him go … any …faster," her voice came out a staccato as her teeth rattled.

Nate laughed. "Faster?"

Did she dare? But how else was she going to face her fear? "Yes!"

Nate laughed again, just as a shot fired.

BOOM!

The blast came from the direction of Bonnie and Bart's place. Jack, on the other hand, was determined to go in the opposite. He lunged at the sound, yanking the reins out of Nate's hands as he did, and took off. Libby screamed and held on. What else could she do? She heard Nate yell after them, but his voice was drowned out by the sound of Jack's thundering hooves.

BOOM!

Libby hung on for dear life, and was surprised when Jack didn't speed up at the sound of the second blast. Instead, he started to slow his pace, and Libby silently thanked God for the miracle. She then heard a loud whistle behind her. Jack obediently came to a stop. Libby shook like a leaf, and hung on as Jack responded to a second whistle, turned around, and trotted back to his master. When they reached Nate, he pulled Libby from the saddle and crushed her against him. "I'm so sorry, sweetheart! That never should have happened! Jack usually doesn't spook like that." He looked down at her as he gently set her on her feet. He'd been holding her so tight they hadn't even touched the ground. "You okay?"

She nodded, unable to speak. On the one hand, she was terrified. On the other, she felt proud of herself for not falling flat on her face.

Nate pulled her into his arms again and held her close. "It's okay sweetheart, you're safe now."

She pushed him away. She didn't want him to think of her as some baby. "I know I am!"

He stared down at her, dumbfounded. "What?"

"I know I'm safe. I'm not a child; you don't have to always coddle me."

He gaped at her. "I'm just trying to protect you, is all! Yesterday you loved it when I held you! Today you don't?"

"It's not that... it's... oh, I don't know what it is!"

She turned to go into the cabin, but he stopped her. He took her by the arms, turned her around to face him, and then claimed her mouth with his own. Another shotgun blast rent the air. Nate held her tighter still.

When he finally broke the kiss, she was panting. "Well, now," Nate drawled. "I do believe my little Libby is growing up." He pushed his hat back. "Don't that beat all?"

Before she could say another word, his mouth descended upon hers once more. Another shot fired, but neither of them paid it any mind.

TEN

Nate Dalton burned.

Burned with a desire he never knew existed. He wanted Libby, wanted her something awful, and if he didn't get her soon, he thought he might die.

When Jack spooked and took off with his wife, a deep fear gripped him. Nate had never experienced anything like it, and for a scant moment, understood her panic as if he were on the horse and not her. It so rattled him, he yelled after the horse instead of whistling, which was what Jack would respond to. Gathering his wits about him, he finally did, and Jack, God bless him, obeyed as he'd been trained, and brought his Libby back. Nate pulled her off the saddle and held her as if their very lives depended on it, then was shocked when she scolded him for it. Yet, wasn't that what he was after? Getting his wife to fight back? Show a little gumption? Of course it was. The only problem now was that he was more attracted to her than ever.

Nate looked at her, still in his arms, and fought a wave of passion. "Libby," he rasped. "We should go inside."

She stared blankly back. "Huh?"

He smiled. By God if he hadn't kissed her senseless! About time! Unable to help himself, he scooped her up into his arms and headed for the cabin's front door.

"What are you doing?" she yelped in surprise.

"I think it's about time I carried you across the threshold, don't you?"

Libby laughed, the sound sending a tingle up his spine, not to mention a few other places. He'd better decide right now what he was going to do. He wanted to woo her proper, win her over, and make her desire him with every fiber of her being. If he took her now, she'd be confused. He wanted her sure of her feelings for him, wanted their desire to be mutual.

Of course, he knew he could seduce her easily enough, but he didn't want that with Libby. He wanted her heart and soul, not just her body. He'd been on the other end of that all his life. Women were easy for the Dalton men to get when they wanted one. Their looks alone achieved it. But he didn't want Libby to just desire him; he wanted Libby to adore him and chase after his heart as much as he wanted to chase after hers. He hadn't realized it until he and Walt headed out to check another fence line that morning. Bart got the pleasure of driving his wife and her sisters to town, and Nate realized he was jealous he'd been appointed the task. He wanted to spend more time with Libby and, dagnabit, Bart got the pleasure and not Nate! At least he got to come home early and spend time with her now. Maybe too much time…

"I can fix you a sandwich," she breathed, her lips still pink and swollen from his kiss.

His mouth opened as his head lowered and he stopped himself. *Not now, Dalton!* He

thought. *You've not won her completely.* "Sounds wonderful, darlin'." He let her go and noted the look of disappointment on her face.

"I'll… just go fix us something."

"You do that, and I'll take care of Jack."

She nodded, her eyes reluctant to leave his.

He smiled at her, tweaked her nose, and winked. "I'll see you in a little while, Mrs. Dalton."

She blushed from head to toe, and he stifled a groan. His whole body tightened, and if he had any sense at all, he'd toss himself into the horse trough.

"Are you all right?" she asked.

He couldn't answer right away, his jaw so tight his teeth were grinding.

"You look funny," she commented as she studied him.

"It's nothing," he said, his voice coming out a croak.

She eyed him and cocked her head to one side. "Are you sick?"

"Good Lord, she hit the nail on the head! He *was* sick. Love sick! How did this happen? He wanted her, desired her and, in that moment, it was all he could do to keep his hands off of her! Sure, he wanted her to desire him just as much and even more. Had *he* already gone past more? "I have to take care of Jack," he pushed out through clenched teeth. He then spun on his heel and went to take care of his horse.

Libby watched as Nate hurried to the barn and sighed. Why was Nate acting so funny all of a sudden? She shook the thought off and went inside. The only thing she could think to make was bacon and eggs. She gathered what she needed and set to work. By the time she got the meal ready, Nate came back. It was then she realized he'd been gone quite a while, and turned to face him. "What happened to you?" she gasped.

"Dunked my head in the horse trough," he said as he strode to the table, his head and shoulders dripping.

"The horse trough? Why would you do that?"

"I was… hot. It's hot outside, you know."

Libby's eyes flicked to the window. "Not that hot …"

"Hot enough," he said. "Is that bacon?"

Libby nodded, fixed his plate, and set it on the table. "I'll have you know, I didn't burn a thing."

He looked at her as he absently brushed water off his face. "Really? This calls for a celebration!"

Libby smiled, and stood behind him and put her arm around his neck. Feeling bold, she rested her cheek atop his head. He stiffened at the action. Didn't he want her to be affectionate? Maybe his earlier kiss was just that, a simple kiss, and nothing more. Perhaps that's what the others were as well. Her heart sank with the thought. Nate still didn't feel a wit of anything for her. She backed away and returned to the stove. "I can make more if you like."

She listened as he began to eat. "This is fine."

She took a deep breath and let it out slowly, so he wouldn't hear it, then fixed her own plate and sat.

They ate in silence, and as soon as Nate was done he got up and snatched his hat off the peg near the door. "Where are you going?"

"To have a word with my brother."

"Which one?"

"Bart. I'll be back soon." He then left.

What was wrong with him? One minute he had her moaning in his arms, the next he acted as if he didn't want anything to do with her! Libby rolled her eyes in frustration. "I have got to talk to Bonnie!"

Speaking of Bonnie, Libby needed to store the few sewing supplies she'd purchased, and wondered if Nate had a container or a box she could use. She glanced around the kitchen and living room, but didn't see anything, so continued her search in the bedroom. In the week since their arrival, Libby had studied and nosed around every nook and cranny in the cabin, except one.

Nate's trunk.

She stared at it, and wondered if she dare open it. She didn't ask Nate if she could, after all, and maybe he kept things tucked away in there for a reason. The reason being, he didn't what anyone to see certain... *things.* After all, that's what Libby and her sisters used trunks for. They hid things in them all the time. Libby giggled at the thought as she knelt before the trunk. She undid the latch and opened it. He hadn't told her *not* to open it, either.

"Hmm, nothing much exciting about more blankets." She took them out and set them to the side. What lay underneath wasn't any more interesting. There was a bridle, a nice one too; black with silver buckles polished to a high sheen. "Let's see, what else..." A pair of spurs, a cigar box—naturally she peeked, but it just had some receipts and papers, so she immediately closed it up—a few books, a shirt, and... "What's that?"

Libby moved the shirt aside and stared at the oddity. She picked it up and studied it. "Oh, I know what this is!" Libby giggled. Nate Dalton was the proud owner of a boy's slingshot. Benedict, Hank and Percy had all had one when they were boys, and she could remember hitting Percy in the ankle with a rock when she was seven. Her aim was a shock to her brothers, and just as amusing, at least to Bert and Hank. Percy, on the other hand, did not share in their amusement, nor did he to this day. He still had the scar.

Libby stood and studied the toy, even though, according to her brothers and father, a slingshot was no mere toy. In her hands, at the time, Percy had announced it a lethal weapon! She laughed out loud at the memory, and recalled the look on Percy's face when her antics had sent him hopping into a nearby horse trough! Only, Percy didn't get just his head and shoulders wet as Nate had earlier. He fell in, went under, and came up spitting mad. Libby had dropped the slingshot and taken off at a run for the mercantile. She thought if she hid from him long enough, he'd calm down. She'd hoped so, anyway.

Libby giggled, put the slingshot and other things back in the trunk, closed the lid, and covered it up with the shirt. "What am I to put my sewing supplies in?"

Perhaps Gwen would have something she could use. She looked at the trunk again. If she had been thinking, she'd have kept out the cigar box. She could use it as a small sewing box until she got one in Wiggieville. Of course, she'd ask Nate first if she could use it.

Speaking of her husband, he should be back any time. How long did it take to walk over to Bart and Bonnie's and talk a few moments? Unless they were talking about something serious. Her guess was he went to go see what the earlier shooting was about. But what if it was more than that? What if he went to his brother's house to complain about her? To tell him he didn't want to be married to a nothing of a girl?

"But I'm not a girl," she whispered to herself. "I'm as much a woman as my sisters… I think." She had to talk to Bonnie! She had so many questions now about love, life, and men. Who else was she going to ask? If this had anything to do with dresses or the latest hair fashion, she could ask Gwen. Bonnie wasn't much use in that category. But Libby could no more ask Gwen about love than she could Bonnie about fashion. "I'll have to wait and speak with her tomorrow," she mused aloud. "Maybe then I'll find out what I should do." Libby sidestepped around the trunk and sat on the bed. 'What *am* I going to do? What if Nate doesn't… love me?"

Libby sat, eyes wide, as she realized that she might be falling in love.

"But what happens if he doesn't love me back?" For now, that question would go un- answered. In the meantime, she'd occupy her thoughts with what to make her husband for supper later, and hoped she didn't fall in love with him any more than she already had.

Over an hour had passed since Nate left Libby to speak to his brother. When he reached Bart's cabin and he smelled meat cooking, he decided to give Bart and Bonnie a chance to have their supper in private. He knew how he'd feel if someone interrupted his meal, and so took a stroll onto the prairie to clear his head. "I have to be gentle," he mused aloud as he walked. "Gentle, yet firm." That was how to handle his little Libby. But how was he going to handle himself? The moment she snuggled against him when they went to bed, he might go mad! How was he going to hold out? Dunking his head in a horse trough worked once, but he didn't want to make it a habit.

But wait… what if he was so tuckered out at the end of the day that he was too tired to even think about… Yes! That's what he'd do. He'd make sure he was so worn out there was no chance he'd have the energy or wherewithal to be tempted by his wife!

The thought settled in his mind. He'd already tried to pretend to be tired, just so she wouldn't worry about him making any untoward advances. Now he really would be. Nate smiled and whistled as he strolled across the prairie.

One hour later—and a discussion with his brother—Nate was on his way home. The conversation with Bart had put him in a less-than-congenial mood. Bart was determined to leave on another one of his safaris, and seemed to have no qualms about leaving his wife behind to fend for herself. If the idiot had any sense at all, he'd take Bonnie with him! Of course, if Nate had any sense at all, he'd have brought it up! He rolled his eyes at the thought as he entered the cabin.

Libby was nowhere in sight.

Nate glanced around again. She must be in the bedroom. He went to the bedroom door and gave it a soft knock. "Libby?"

"Yes?" came from the other side of the door.

Nate opened it and walked in. "Hey, darlin', what are you doing?"

"Nothing. I was bored, I guess."

"Bored? I haven't been gone that long."

"I did put on a pot of soup. I thought we could have it with some bread tonight. It should be done soon."

"Sounds fine," he said as he sat on the bed next to her. He stiffened as he met her gaze, and realized where they were. Perhaps sitting together on the bed wasn't such a good idea. "Would you like to go into the other room?"

"Okay."

They stood, and she turned to him. "I was looking for something to put some sewing supplies in, but didn't find anything. Except a cigar box in your trunk," she told him and pointed at the foot of the bed.

"You can use it if you want. I'll get it for you. Why don't you get a sewing box the next time you're in town?"

"That was my plan," she said as she watched him open the trunk and begin to dig through the contents.

"Nice slingshot you have there, by the way."

He stood, the cigar box in his hand, and gave it to her. "Oh, yes… *that*.

She folded her arms across her chest and smiled. "My guess is that, *that* has a story behind it."

Nate felt himself blush. How embarrassing… "Yes, it certainly does."

"I would love to hear all about it," she told him with a grin.

Though she smiled, he could tell something wasn't right. He also knew he needed to get them out of the bedroom. He grabbed the slingshot out of the trunk, closed it, then took her by the hand and led her to the settee in the living area. Once they were settled, he let out a heavy sigh. "Where to begin…"

"You could always tell it to me backwards and then I'd have to piece it together. You know, like a puzzle?"

"You are a silly woman," he told her as he tweaked her nose. "My brothers and I each have one of these."

"Really? When did you get them?"

"We must've been about ten or so when we lived in Oregon City. We got into more trouble with these slingshots than any other toy we'd been given. Caused a stagecoach to go off the road with this."

Libby gasped. "Nate Dalton! You didn't!"

"Yep, though I think Walt was the one who did that; I can't remember. I was the one who knocked a man into a grave, though."

"What?!" she said, eyes wide.

"With a rock. Finn Mullany was his name. He was an undertaker, and had just dug a grave. We all took a shot at the same time, but I'm the only one who hit him."

"That's terrible! Did he get hurt?"

"No, other than a bump on his head. But he was hopping mad. I thought I was going to die that day. Thankfully, I saw a woman walking across his pumpkin patch. The Mullany family grew them for extra money. Anyway, she tripped and fell down, so I started screaming at Finn that he had a woman in his pumpkin patch. He didn't believe me, though."

"What did he do?"

"He threatened to tell my pa what my brothers and I had done. Thankfully, the gal popped up, and he saw her and let me go."

"What happened then?"

He looked at her and smiled. "They got married."

"No, not to him; to you and your brothers. What did your father do when he found out you'd hit the poor man in the head with a rock?"

"Oh, he was mad, and made us give up our slingshots to Mr. Mullany. But we got them back after a week or so. Good thing too. Some scoundrel came to town and caused trouble for the Mullany family. If it weren't for these slingshots, that poor woman from the pumpkin patch would be dead at the worst, scarred at best."

Libby gasped. "Mercy! What happened?"

Nate started to toss the slingshot back and forth in his hands. "We hit the bad guy and knocked him flat. For once, our aim was good."

Libby stared at him, enthralled. "Was this before, or after, they got married?"

"Before," Nate chuckled. "They got married in

that same pumpkin patch. It was really rather romantic, now that I think on it."

Libby smiled again. "Do you... think about romance much?"

He looked at her and swallowed hard. "Not much."

"Oh," she said, her voice low, and turned away.

Nate, you idiot, he thought to himself. He was about to grab her, pull her against him, and kiss her senseless. But he knew what the end result would be, and didn't want her like that. She deserved better. Instead, he did the only thing he could think of. "Is the soup ready yet?"

ELEVEN

The next few days passed in a blur for Libby, and she was surprised she could recall as much of it as she did. Baking bread for the first time without burning it, Gwen did a little dance around her kitchen in front of her and Bonnie. It was a comical sight, and Libby couldn't help but smile and giggle as Gwen pirouetted at the end. She'd mastered the art of bread-baking and was ecstatic over her achievement. Libby mastered it, too, but had been so preoccupied wondering if Nate had any true feelings for her, that she'd almost missed sharing in Gwen's happiness. She was cheating herself out of moments like Gwen's, and decided she didn't want to miss anymore, such as the one they shared the next day; only it wasn't something to dance about.

Libby and Bonnie were at Gwen's house sewing, (Bonnie was sewing, Gwen and Libby were stabbing fabric with needles) trying to make curtains for Bonnie's cabin, when they heard a wagon outside. They looked at each other in apprehension at first. Who could it be? Nate and Walton were out on the prairie somewhere working, and Bart was on a business trip. Bonnie told them about it the day before, and so Gwen asked her to have supper with her and Walt. Libby was planning on inviting her to supper, too, so she wouldn't have to eat alone. Maybe Bart was back already…

Gwen must have had the same thought, because she went to the door and answered it. The person on the other side, however, was most definitely *not* Bart.

Libby and Bonnie craned their necks to see past Gwen. They knew it was a woman, they could at least see part of her skirt. Leaning further for a better view, they could then see that she was a very *pregnant* woman.

Libby and Bonnie's eyes became riveted on the doorway and the two women in it. Libby, for one, had never been so proud of Gwen as she was in that moment.

The woman introduced herself as one Lela Mason; an acquaintance, of sorts, of Walton's. Though, "of sorts" was a gross understatement. She told Gwen she was there to see Walton about… *their baby!*

Libby almost choked upon hearing the word! What sort of life had Walton Dalton led before he married her sister? A better question might be what kind of life had *all three* brothers led before marrying?

No sooner had she thought it, than Gwen shut the door in the woman's face, returned to the table where they'd been working, and sat. "I'll be staying at your house tonight after I have a little *talk* with my husband, Bonnie."

Libby and Bonnie exchanged another look. "Don't you think you should give him a chance to explain?" Bonnie asked.

Gwen looked about to bust a gut! "Absolutely not! Her swollen belly explained everything as far as I'm concerned! How he could be interested in that... that *tart*, I don't know."

Libby's shock grew by the second, but not so much that she didn't scold Gwen for calling her husband something she shouldn't. But who could blame her? What would she or Bonnie do if such a woman showed up on their doorstep? What were the chances that one wouldn't? If it happened to Gwen, it could happen to Libby or Bonnie easily enough. The Dalton Brothers had been single men for a very long time...

Libby's chest tightened with the thought. It was bad enough Gwen had to suffer such a fate. Hadn't she been through enough scandal? But what if the same thing happened to her and Nate? Or worse, to Bonnie while Bart was away? She looked at her sister as she spoke with Gwen. If Bart always left on business, then how faithful was he being to her sister?

Not long after Miss Mason's surprise visit, Bonnie and Libby left. Neither wanted to be there when Walt got home to suffer Gwen's wrath. In what shape or form it came in, they didn't know, but guaranteed it would come.

When they reached Libby's cabin, they gave each other a quick hug and glanced back at Gwen's place. The men would be home soon, and both wondered about the upcoming exchange. "She'll be fine," Bonnie assured. "Just fine. Don't worry, I'll take care of her."

Speechless, Libby could only nod. *What* had

they gotten themselves into?

She went into the cabin and sat at the kitchen table a few moments to collect her thoughts. But then, her thoughts were what caused the dither she'd been in the last few days. Maybe it would be better if she concentrated on making supper for Nate.

She went outside to the root cellar. She'd learn to take a lantern with her so she could see, and gathered what she needed for supper. She then went to the smoke house and did the same. Bonnie told her about a recipe for fried apples and sausage, so Libby thought she'd try it without *any* instruction. It was a brave thing to do, but Libby didn't want to be labeled a coward when it came to cooking. She'd already labeled herself as one in most other areas. She'd never thought herself a coward until she came out west and plunked down in the middle of the Texas prairie. However, her cowardice was quite apparent not only to her, but to everyone around her as well. The question was what she'd do about it.

"Be brave, that's what I'm going to do!" she muttered as she sliced the sausage. "I'll have Nate teach me how to ride, and shoot just like Bart taught Bonnie."

Libby shuddered. She hated loud noises. "Okay, so maybe I'll have him teach me to shoot a *little* gun." She stopped slicing. Tears filled her eyes and her lower lip trembled. *Oh great!* Now she was going to cry? She rubbed her eyes with the back of her hand and forced the tears back. "Oh, what is wrong with me?"

But she knew well what it was. She was afraid Nate had his own Lela Mason tucked away somewhere, one sure to show up on her doorstep one day. "Libby, you dolt, stop thinking about yourself, and think about Gwen! She's the one with the problem, not you!"

She took a deep breath and finished slicing the sausages. She then peeled and sliced the apples. She had no idea how this was going to turn out, but was willing to give it a try. After she fried up the sausages and apples, she put them in one of her new pans and set them in the warming oven. She then sliced up a couple of potatoes to fry. By the time they were done, Nate stepped into the cabin.

He hung up his hat and coat and joined her at the stove. "What smells so good?"

She forced herself not to look at him. "I'm trying something new."

He put his arms around her waist and held her close. She stiffened, but then, so did he. Was he forcing himself to hold her? She closed her eyes and bit her lip. *Oh please, Lord,* she prayed. *Is that why he's distant? Does he have a woman tucked away somewhere that I don't know about?* "Supper's ready," she told him in an even tone, and tried to pull out of his embrace.

He released her and went to the sideboard to get their plates. "What did your sister teach you today?"

Libby swallowed hard as she watched him. He was tall, strong, and handsome. Everything a woman could want in a man, as far as looks went. But he was also kind, patient, gentle, and good at relieving her fears of late. But she wasn't sure how he was going to relieve this one. This one had a name, and there were possibly others. What if Lela Mason had sisters, and they'd had trysts with Walt's brothers?

Nate turned around. "Darlin'..." he began in a warning tone. "You've got that look in your eye."

Libby straightened. "What look is that?"

"The one that says you've been chewing on something *way too hard* all day, and worked yourself up over it." He brought the plates to the table and set them down. "What happened?"

"Uh... nothing." She rubbed her hands on her skirt a few times then took a seat.

Nate watched her a moment, and smiled. "Aren't you forgetting something?"

"What?" she asked and pulled a plate toward her.

"Um... dishing up our supper?"

Libby's eyes grew round as saucers. "Oh! Yes, of course. No, I didn't forget... really."

"Really?" Nate drawled as he crossed his arms over his chest. "Libby Dalton, what is it this time?"

She popped up from the chair and went to the stove. She took the pan of sausage and apples from the warming oven and brought it to the table. She then quickly dished them each a portion. "Nothing at all." She returned to the stove and set down the pan.

"Libby..."

With the dishrag she'd used to take the pan out of the warming oven, she grabbed the potatoes, brought them to the table, and added some to each plate. Without thinking, she looked at her husband. He wasn't glaring at her, but he wasn't smiling either. "What?"

His eyes raked over her and he balled his hands into fists. She must've upset him. But so what? He didn't have to know every little thing that went on in her head! Besides, he really didn't want to know what was in her head now!

She went to the stove and slammed the pan onto it. She then spun on her heel, stomped to the table and sat. "Do you want to pray or shall I?"

His mouth dropped half open. He then snapped it shut and took his seat. "Go right ahead."

Libby slapped her hands together. "Dear Lord, bless this food and the hands that provided it. And Lord, please help my sister try not to kill her husband. Amen."

This time Nate's mouth dropped open like he had a rock tied to his jaw. "What?!"

"You heard me."

"Yeah, I heard you, but I don't understand what you're saying. Gwen's gonna kill Walt?"

"That's what I said."

Nate shook himself, blinked a few times, and then gawked at her. "Why would Gwen want to kill Walt?"

"Well, wouldn't you if someone from your past showed up on your doorstep?"

Nate could only stare at her a moment. "What are you talking about?"

"I'm talking about the pregnant woman who showed up on your brother's doorstep this afternoon."

Nate sat, dumbfounded, and didn't say a word.

That's all it took to convince Libby there was some semblance of truth to her imaginings. All three brothers had someone in their past to hide. She grabbed her plate and stood. "I'm going to dine in the bedroom, if you don't mind." With that, she spun on her heel and left the kitchen.

Nate sat in stunned silence. It took him a moment to collect himself, but when he did…

"What in Sam Hill is going on around here?" he slammed his fist on the table.

"Dagnabit, fool woman! What does she think she's doing?"

A muffled, "I heard that!" came from the other side of the bedroom door.

Nate narrowed his eyes, grabbed his plate—he was hungry after all; got up and marched straight for the bedroom. "Libby!" he shouted. You open this door! Remember what I told you about locking doors?"

"Open it yourself; it's not locked," she said from the other side.

Nate rolled his eyes in response. It hadn't occurred to him to try the door first. He entered, plate in hand. "Would you like to explain to me what all that was about?"

"Certainly," she said and took a bite of fried apple. She chewed thoughtfully a moment then swallowed. "A pregnant woman showed up on Gwen's doorstep today, looking for your brother. What do you know about it?"

"Nothing!"

"Really?"

"Did she give a name?"

"Lela Mason. It wouldn't sound familiar, would it?"

"No."

THE COWBOY'S MAIL-ORDER BRIDE   149

Her expression changed, but only for a moment. She was putting up a brave front, he could tell, and was upset for good reason. If a woman like that showed up on his doorstep with her sisters here, he was sure they'd be beside themselves as well. He, of course, would be a dead man. An image of Gwen shooting Walt crossed his mind, and Nate briefly wondered how his brother fared at the moment. But this was Walt's problem, not his. Besides, he knew Walt always figured some disgruntled female would try to get her hooks in him somehow. Word had spread of their ranch already, even as small as it was, and the brothers had discussed the possibility of gold-diggers.

"Is that what has you upset? Some woman trying to see what she can get out of my brother? You know that's all there is to it, don't you?"

She looked at the floor, then back again. "How are we supposed to know anything? We've only been here a little over a week!"

"Exactly. Which means, for all I know, you have twenty beaus back east all catching trains at this very moment, to come carry you back with them; it's only a matter of which one gets here first!"

She picked at her dress. "Gwen, maybe, but never me," she sighed. "Or Bonnie for that matter."

"Well then," he said as he sat next to her on the bed. "Looks like Walt's going to have his hands full. But I tell you truly, none of us would ever, and I do mean *ever*, do such a thing to a woman, you understand?"

"How would you know if you did?" She looked at him with a combination of fear and hope. Fear, that he'd say they wouldn't. Hope, that he'd say...

"We know, because we're, well, careful. Besides, none of us associates ourselves with those kinds of women."

Her eyes went blank. "Careful? What do you mean by, careful?"

"Oh for Heaven's sakes," he muttered to himself. "Careful means, at least for me, that I'm not going to just bed a woman then forget about it. I want it to mean something. Now, eat your supper," he snapped.

Her eyes went wide, and then she quickly collected herself. "Fine!" She stood and went back to the kitchen. He followed her without a word, and they both sat at the table and finished the meal in silence.

When they were done eating, he went to start a fire while Libby did the dishes. She hadn't made anything for dessert that evening. But for Nate, a cup of coffee would do. In fact, maybe he'd have a cup and go take a walk or something. He was irritated. Irritated that she still didn't trust him, and irritated with Walt that he didn't make it clear to whomever this Lela Mason was, that he wasn't interested in her at the time they'd met, wherever that was, though he was sure Walt would tell her now. And finally, he was irritated with Bart for taking off on safari and leaving his wife alone! So far, he and his brothers weren't doing a very good job at this marriage business.

But he wasn't the one to keep Libby from her fears. She was going to have to face them, one by one. All he could do was stand by her side as she did, then comfort and hold her until she was ready to face the next one. Once overcome, she could help him with his.

Nate's biggest, he realized, was that she would never grow to love him. They'd be just two people sharing a house, a bed, some meals, and nothing more. That one thought scared Nate Dalton to death.

He got the fire going, stood, and turned to see if Libby had put on a pot of coffee. She had. He'd been so wrapped up in his own frustrations he hadn't heard her do it. But where was she?

He went to the bedroom, but she wasn't there. He then looked at the front door, and noticed her shawl was missing. Stepping to the window, he looked outside and, sure enough, she stood in front of the cabin and stared into the distance.

Nate closed his eyes, bowed his head, and sent up a silent prayer that he and his brothers didn't do something stupid enough to lose the one good thing they had in their lives right now.

Their wives.

TWELVE

The next day brought about a series of events that would change Libby's life forever. Of course, the night before hadn't helped to get things off to a good start. She'd put on a pot of coffee then gone outside for a few moments to collect her thoughts, unable to stand being in the cabin with Nate any longer. He didn't love her, that was for certain, otherwise wouldn't he have taken her and... Oh, wait a minute. No, he wouldn't. She was the one who wanted him to woo her before they made love. But the only reason she did was so he'd love her before they *made* love!

A lot of good it did her now.

The man could woo and not love at the same time. Libby, in her naivety, assumed one could not be done without the other. How stupid could she have been? She stared at the moon and cried last night until she knew she'd better go inside before Nate came out. She might as well let him have his way with her now. He wasn't going to love her anyway. Maybe he was just trying to please her, so she'd do well with her cooking and sewing lessons. Who knew?

Men! How could they possibly be with a woman and not love her? Libby just didn't get it.

She then realized she had another problem. Nate wasn't going to love her after he wooed her. She, on the other hand, could very well already be in love with him. But how could she be sure? What if what ailed her was perfectly curable? What if it wasn't?

Libby knew of only one way to find out. Ask Bonnie.

However, before she could do that, she'd have to get through the rest of the day. A day that consisted of none other than Lela Mason showing up on Gwen's doorstep again! But this time, things were different.

Gwen answered the door, while Libby and Bonnie waited for her to give the woman her due. A swift kick in the rear, perhaps? But instead of a fight breaking out, the woman shocked them with her words, "I'm sorry."

Come to find out, Lela sought out Walton because she was desperate, and knew he was a good man. Her hope was that he'd help her out by marrying her. She created a ruse to trap him into it, only to come to the ranch and discover he was already married. She'd lost her job—albeit that of a whore, and had nowhere to go except the one person she thought could help. Libby and Bonnie half expected Gwen to still throw the woman out on her ear. But Gwen took them by surprise with what she did. She offered to help the woman!

Before Libby and Bonnie knew it, Lela Mason was helping them sew Bonnie's curtains! Who would've ever thought? But what really hit Libby was the fact that the woman did what she did because Walt Dalton was a good man; the only one she trusted enough to help her in her hour of need. If a woman such as Lela Mason could trust Walt Dalton to help her in such a dire situation, couldn't Libby trust Nate to love her in time?

Libby stole quick glances at Bonnie all morning. Bart was off on a business trip, and could be gone for a week. Bonnie trusted *him*, didn't she? Perhaps they were already in love! She could tell Gwen was in love with her husband, or at least falling fast. At least until Lela had knocked on the door. But if she didn't love him, would it have been as easy for her to forgive Lela? Besides, wouldn't forgiving Lela make it easier for Gwen to forgive Walt? Of course, then she'd have to forgive herself for not trusting him in the first place.

Libby bit her lip as the other women talked and sewed. Was she the only one who didn't trust her husband? She glanced at Bonnie again, and decided she would speak to her later that day. In the meantime, Lela needed their help, and any woman who had the guts enough to do what she did to protect her child had Libby's respect, not to mention that of her sisters. She pushed her own troubles aside, and chimed in with suggestions on how to help Lela start a new life.

The four women had sewn and talked for several hours before Walt came home. Libby was gratified when he made up with Gwen and all was forgiven. Tomorrow, they would help Lela find a place to stay and figure out what she could do in order to support herself until she married. Gwen was sure there were plenty of men in town willing to take on her and her unborn child, women being exceedingly scarce. Because of that, they would also be willing to overlook her past employment. In Beckham, a former whore would be shunned, no matter if God's light shined down on her or not. Folks back east were not so forgiving, it seemed, as those in Texas.

Speaking of forgiving ...

Some time later, she knocked on Bonnie's door.

"Libby," Bonnie said in surprise as she opened it. "What are you doing here?"

"I needed to talk to you before Nate gets home."

"Is something wrong?" her sister asked as she stepped aside to let Libby in.

"Oh, Bonnie..." Libby said as several tears fell. "Everything's wrong!"

"What do you mean, everything? I thought the two of you were..." For a moment Bonnie froze, as though she couldn't speak. She cleared her throat. "I thought the two of you were fine."

"We're not. Nate doesn't love me. But I think I'm in love with him. And if I'm in love with him and he doesn't love me... I don't know how I'm going to live!"

"Live?"

"I didn't say that right," Libby lamented and threw a hand in the air in frustration. "What I mean is, I don't know how I can live my life married to a man who doesn't love me. It would be easier if I wasn't in love with him, I suppose, but ... I think I am. Am I making any sense?" Libby's words came out in a rush.

Bonnie sidestepped to the only chair, and sat. "I'd like to say, not any more than usual, but in this case you make perfect sense."

Libby pulled up the crate and sat next to her. "You're in love with Bart. What's it like?"

"Like?" Bonnie almost choked on the word.

"Yes, what does it feel like? Maybe if I knew the symptoms, I'd be able to tell if I was in love with Nate or not."

"Don't you *want* to be in love with him?" Bonnie asked.

"Well, of course, if he's going to love me, which he doesn't."

"What makes you think he doesn't?"

Libby thought a moment. "Remember when I told you I made him sleep on the floor on my wedding night, and that he'd have to woo me? Well, he *did* try to woo me. I think he's still trying."

"Then what's the problem?"

"That's just it. He's only wooing me. There's nothing else along with it. He's wooing me and making me fall in love with him, but what am I doing to make him fall in love with me? Nothing! Except burn his meals, and what man falls in love with that?"

Bonnie put her face in her hands and groaned. "Oh, Libby." She pulled her face out of her hands and looked at her. "Libby, Libby, Libby," she repeated. "That's not what love is about."

"Then what *is* it about?"

Bonnie drew in a deep breath and let it out slowly. "Well, it's about doing things for him that you maybe don't want to do, but you're going to do them anyway, because you care about him. It's about being alongside him day in and day out, not always because you want to, but because it's the right place to be. It's about taking care of his home and having pride in your work. Part of it's for you, yes, but also for him. It's putting your trust in him, Libby, knowing that he has your best interests in mind and that you can count on him."

"What about a man doing things for you? Like, falling at your feet? That's how Gwen used to tell if a boy liked her."

Bonnie laughed and shook her head. "That is *not* how you tell. Besides, Gwen now

knows the difference."

"But I'm not Gwen," Libby told her.

"No, you're not. Maybe knowing if you're in love is a little different for everybody."

"Then how am I going to know if I am?"

Bonnie took another deep breath. "For you, little sister, I think it's knowing that Nate cherishes you."

"Cherishes me?"

"Yes. I know you, Libby, and I know that if Nate is protecting you, sheltering you, keeping you warm and safe ... well then, he's cherishing you and taking care of you. In other words, he's making you the most important thing in his world. Sure, a lot of men do it out of duty because it's the right thing to do. But then there are men who go above and beyond and..." she suddenly stopped.

"Bonnie? Are you all right?"

Bonnie's jaw went slack a moment, her eyes wide. She then quickly collected herself and looked at Libby. "What does Nate do when he's with you? Is he affectionate?"

"Oh, yes."

"Does he want to spend time with you?"

"Well, yes, but…"

"Do you want to spend time with him?"

Libby clasped her hands in her lap. "All the time."

"So you miss him during the day when he's out working?"

Libby nodded. She did, now that she thought on it. There hadn't been a day since her arrival she didn't think of him, wondered if he was warm enough, or if he was hungry.

"Oh, my… I think, I'm…"

"In love with your husband?" Bonnie finished.

"I *am* in love with him!" she looked at Bonnie, horrified. "This is terrible!" She got up and raced for the door.

"Libby!" Bonnie called after her. "Where are you going?"

"Home. I have to find out if he loves me, too!"

"Libby!"

Libby turned, the door already open. "What?"

"I can guarantee you that he does."

Libby chewed her lower lip. "That may be so, but I have to hear the words from him for myself." With that, she left.

Libby raced to her cabin, and had no sooner reached it than Nate rode up. "Libby, darlin', what's wrong? Is there a fire?" He quickly dismounted and went to her. "Are you all right?"

Libby gazed into his eyes and saw the familiar

concern there; the same he had for her whenever he thought something wasn't right. The look was there every time she'd been out of sorts, and the day Jack galloped away with her. It had always been there. But she thought it meant something else. She thought it meant a task on his part. She was something to be taken care of, so that he could move on to other things, more important things, like his chores out at the barn or his work on the range. But that wasn't it at all. In truth, she had compared him to her father and hadn't realized it.

For her father, having to deal with one of Gwen's escapade's or Bonnie's failure to obtain a husband, and of course Libby's own shortcomings, was a chore. A task he had to deal with and quickly, lest it mar his sterling reputation. The thought sickened her, and Libby realized she had completely misjudged her new husband. She wasn't a nuisance to him or some job. She was his wife, and he was trying to help her ease into the role.

Shame hit Libby hard and fast, and she turned away from him.

"Hey now, darlin," he said softly. "Come here." He gently brushed her cheek with a finger. She turned around to face him. "Talk to me," he coaxed.

Libby swallowed hard. "I will, but… can we go inside?"

"Of course," he said. He tethered Jack to the hitching post and followed her into the cabin. He took off his hat and coat, and then motioned toward the settee. Once they were seated, he put his arm around her and looked into her eyes. "What troubles you, Libby?

Tell me."

She swallowed hard. "You're not mad at me for anything, are you? Like… last night?"

"I admit I was a little. Sometimes I just can't make sense of you, woman."

"That's okay," she said with a weak smile. "I can't make sense of me either."

He blinked at her a couple of times, then laughed. "There's my little Libby," he chuckled. "Now, what's the problem?"

"You're so quick to recover from being angry," she said and looked away. "I've had so many different feelings since we got married, that I haven't been able to sort them out."

He drew her closer, put his other arm around her, and rested his chin atop her head. "That's okay, darlin', I've been having a lot of different feelings, too."

He kissed her hair. A chill went up her spine as warmth settled deep in the pit of her stomach. "What… what kind of feelings?"

"Well, they're kind of hard for a man to explain, but I'll do my best." He shifted, drawing her in closer. "I don't like being away from you during the day while I'm working. So I work harder so I can come home sooner."

Libby pulled away and looked at him. "You do?"

"Yep, I sure do. And even though the first few times you cooked for me, I was afraid it was going to kill me, I ate it anyway to show you my appreciation for the work you put in."

"I thought it was because I'd didn't do as badly as Gwen."

"Oh, trust me, honey; you both did pretty bad at first. Walton and I had our share of belly aches the first few tries."

She hesitated, even though he made a joke and tried to lighten the mood. She picked at her dress. One of his hands covered hers to make her stop. Libby looked into his eyes in response. "Nate?"

"What, darlin'?" he asked, his voice soft as he leaned toward her.

"If I ask you something, will you tell me the truth?"

"I've never lied to you, Libby. I'm not gonna start now. Does this have anything to do with that woman who showed up at Walt's yesterday?"

"Not anymore," she said as she now leaned in his direction.

"Then, what is it?" he asked, their faces inches apart.

Libby swallowed hard. "Do you love me?"

He drew back a few inches. "Do I *love* you?" Their eyes locked. "Do I love you?" he repeated.

She looked at him and could scarcely breathe.

He reached up and cupped her face with a hand. "Do I love you?" he whispered. "Do I?" The words were spoken against her lips. "Do I love you, Libby?" he whispered as his mouth took hers. He drew her into his arms, and kissed her with a passion she had not yet experienced. His hands roamed her body as he deepened the kiss, one that caused her heart to pound in her chest like a herd of wild horses. When their lips parted, he whispered against her ear, "Do I love you, Libby? Do I?" He nibbled her earlobe and traced kisses down her neck. "Do I, Libby?" She tilted her head back as his mouth worked its magic across her neck to the other side. "Do I, darlin'?" He drew back and gave her a hungry look. "And what about you? Do you love me?"

Libby's mouth went dry. She still hadn't recovered from his recent onslaught! She studied his face, mouth, eyes, everything there was about him in a single moment. "I do."

Nate's lips curved into a tiny smile. He pulled her against him, closed the distance that remained, and kissed her with everything he had. If Libby had had any doubt in her mind about Nate's feelings for her before, she had *none* now.

In one swift move, he pulled her onto his lap and held tight, never once breaking the kiss. However, a man's gotta breathe. He pushed them apart, his breathing ragged; hers no better. "Nate!" she cried. "What are you doing to me?"

"Loving you, Libby; I'm loving you." He stood with her in his arms, kissed her again, and when they were once more out of breath, carried his bride to the bedroom. Nate Dalton then showed his wife *exactly* how much he loved her.

EPILOGUE

The Dalton Ranch, Christmas day, 1888

Walton Dalton sat at the head of the dinner table, and gazed with pride at his achievements. He and his two brothers, Nate and Bart, had accomplished a feat that would take most men years to do.

They'd built an empire.

Small though it was, it would grow. In fact, it already had. His wife, Gwen, was with child, and he couldn't be happier. Now his brothers would have to play catch up, or forever be jealous.

"That was a fine meal, Libby, Gwen," Nate told them with a nod as he patted his stomach. "I don't know when I've eaten as much."

"And to think we had no help from Bonnie!" Gwen added with a smile.

Walt leaned over and kissed her on the cheek. "You're a wonderful cook. I can't wait for you to teach our ... well, whatever it is we're having."

"Even if it's a boy?" asked Bart from the other end of the table.

"Even if it's a boy," Walt said with a smile.

Libby fidgeted in her chair, but said nothing. The men talked a lot about Walt and Gwen's good fortune. She glanced at Bonnie, and saw that she looked just as uncomfortable with the subject.

"Who's ready for dessert?" Bonnie asked, only to get the men to talk about something else.

"You know I am!" said Walt and Bart in unison.

Everyone went still for a moment, before all six burst into laughter. In fact, they were laughing so hard, no one noticed at first when the door was thrown open.

Walt was the first to snap his mouth shut and come halfway out of his chair. "What the…" He froze as the distinct sounds of shotguns being cocked caught everyone's attention.

Three men stood just inside Nate and Libby's cabin, looking very angry. But not as angry as Gwen, "Benedict! What are you doing here?" she screeched.

Walt's eyes flicked between his wife and the man he figured had to be this Benedict. He was the only one making direct eye contact with her.

Bonnie's mouth dropped open shock. "Hank?"

Now it was Bart's turn to gawk. He narrowed his eyes at the man in the middle, and then slowly turned to look at Bonnie. "Who the hel…"

"Percy?" Libby squeaked at the same time, as she sank a few inches in her chair.

The Dalton brothers were caught off guard. They had no guns at the ready, no weapons… and the fact that their wives *knew* these men was the most disarming of all!

"Get 'em up," demanded Benedict. "Now!"

The Dalton brothers exchanged a quick glance. They were at a distinct disadvantage, so did as he said, and raised their hands in the air.

"Gwen, Libby, Bonnie," snapped Hank, the one in the middle, "get over here. We're going home."

Bonnie closed her eyes tight, opened them, and stood. "Hank? What in Heaven's name are you doing here?"

Bart stared at the newcomer. "Hank?" he mouthed, his face contorted in confusion.

"We might ask you the same question!" snapped the third man, Percy.

"If you must know," Gwen began, "we live here!"

"Yes, we can see that," Benedict said as he took a threatening step forward, "and it looks mighty cozy."

Libby sat up, her face red. "You can't take us back! You just can't!"

"Take you back?" Nate said, his hands balling into fists. "What are you talking about? Who are these men?"

"We'd like to know the same about you!" snapped Percy as he raised his shotgun a little higher.

"I don't care who you are!" barked Walt. "You're trespassing; get off our land!"

"You're hardly in a position to demand anything," Hank pointed out. "All we want are these women."

"Yeah, they've caused us a lot of trouble the last few months!" added Benedict.

"How could we?" asked Gwen. "We've been here the whole time!"

"Precisely, which is why we've come to fetch you and take you back to where and whom you belong," Percy said as he aimed his gun at Nate's heart.

"Percy! Don't!" Libby cried.

"Don't what? Shoot this scum for running off with ya? Or was it the other way around?"

Bonnie squared her shoulders. "Enough!"

"Enough of what, Bonnie?" Hank demanded. "You three have put the family through *enough*!"

"Shut up, all of you!" Bart shouted above the stranger's tantrum.

"I say we hang these scum," suggested Percy.

All three sisters were now on their feet. "NO!"

And then, all hell broke loose...

Walt shoved Gwen behind him as Bart lunged for the nearest man. Libby disappeared completely under the table, whether she was pushed under by Nate or she dove, no one knew, she was just gone. Bonnie stood frozen, and watched in horror as her husband fought for control of Benedict's shotgun. And for Bonnie, Gwen, and Libby (wherever she was), time stood still.

A terrified Libby watched the mad scramble of booted feet rush here and there from her vantage point under the table. Nate pushed her down the moment Bart lunged at one of her brothers. How did Benedict, Hank, and Percy find them? Of course, Hank had to have told their father they'd run away, or maybe spilled the beans that Bonnie had enlisted the help of a mail-order bride service. Not that it mattered now. What did, was keeping her husband alive! Though, she'd have to do the same for her brothers as well.

She crawled to the end of the table, glanced at Gwen tucked into a corner, and grabbed a knife off of Walt's plate. She then crawled back to the fray, and stabbed the first boot to come within range.

Unfortunately, it was Nate's. "OW!" She watched as he hopped on one foot for a second, and then dodged something, probably one of her brothers' fists, but whose?

She scooted to the edge of the table to risk a better view. For whatever reason, the guns were nowhere to be seen, and the men were now engaged in a fist-fight. Of course, she didn't think her big brothers would really shoot Nate or his brothers, but they weren't past using them to get what they wanted! And now they were trying to prove how tough they were, just as they always did. Was it any wonder she and her sisters ran away?

Bart landed next to her on the floor with an audible thud. "Libby! You okay?" But before she could answer, someone pulled him to his feet.

Libby began to back further under the table when … BLAM!

Every boot within Libby's line of vision stopped.

She crawled forward a few inches, and peeked out again. Bonnie had a shotgun in her hand, and Libby had a new hole in her roof. Sensing she'd best help Bonnie, Libby climbed out from under the table.

"Sit down, all of you!" Bonnie demanded.

"Put that gun away before you shoot somebody!" Benedict barked at her.

"That's a good idea; maybe I oughta," she said as she swung the barrel in his direction.

Benedict's hands went up, as did Walt's, who stood next to him.

Gwen came out from the safety of the corner. "Walt! She's not going to shoot you!"

Walt reached up and touched the growing lump on his head, shook his head to clear it, then pulled Gwen into his arms. "Who are you?" he asked the men.

"We're the Blue brothers," said Hank. "And we've come to take our sisters home."

"Brothers?" asked Nate. He grabbed Libby to him. "You never said you had brothers."

"And our sisters never said they were leaving," added Percy.

"Leaving?" began Bart. "What do ya mean, leaving?"

"He means our sisters ran out on a scandal caused by Gwen," Benedict told him. "To alleviate any further damage to the family name, our father painstakingly chose a husband for each of them."

"Yeah, and how do they show their appreciation?" snapped Percy. "By running away!"

"Pa sent us here to bring you back. Deacons Smith, Jackson, and Belafonte paid a tidy sum for us to do it, too."

"But you can't take us back!" Gwen cried.

"And why not?" asked Benedict as he inched toward Bonnie.

"Because we're all married, that's why!" Bonnie announced and raised the gun higher.

Benedict stopped. "We figured that might happen, but those old Deacons don't care. They want you three like fleas want a dog."

Libby and Gwen gasped. "If you're thinking that we're getting annulments, you're sadly mistaken."

"It's been done before," said Percy. "I just hope these scum haven't dishonored you beyond repair."

Gwen rolled her eyes and shook her head. "They've done nothing of the sort. In fact, I'm not only married, I'm expecting!"

Benedict's eyes went straight to her belly, as did his brother's. "You're lying."

"No, I'm not," she said firmly.

"So what if we only bring back two," said Percy. "Two out of three isn't bad!"

"Oh, no you won't!" Libby cried.

"And why not?" demanded Hank.

"Because ..." she looked up at Nate. "I'm going to have a baby, too."

Nate blanched. "What?! You are? Good God, Libby, are ya sure?"

"Yeah, are ya sure?" asked Benedict, who, at this point, looked even paler than Nate did.

"I'm sure," she said, and put her arms around him.

"Libby, my little Libby ..."

Walt and Gwen exchanged a quick glance. Libby was *pregnant?!*

Percy's mouth dropped open in shock at the display. He spun to Bonnie. "Looks like it's just you, Bonnie Blue."

"I don't know what Deacon Smith paid you to bring us back, but I'm not going."

"Put the gun down, Bonnie," Hank said, his voice low. "Let's talk about this. We can't go back empty-handed."

"Why not?" she asked, and pointed the shotgun at him.

"Because …"

"Quiet!" snapped Percy. "Let's just take her and go."

"You're not taking my wife anywhere," hissed Bart. "Bonnie, give me that gun."

"No."

Everyone stared at her in shock. "What?" asked Bart.

"I said, no. These are our brothers, Bart, and they wouldn't be acting so desperate without a good reason."

"I'll not let them take you …"

"You don't have to. I can't go, either."

Bart took a step toward her. "Bonnie …"

"…because I'm expecting, too."

"What?" Gwen and Libby cried in unison. "Bonnie!"

"Bonnie?" Bart echoed, his face pale.

"So you see, my dear brothers, you've failed, as far as taking us back. Now the only question I have for you is, what are you *really* doing here?"

"We have a hole in the roof," Libby stated as she and Nate lay in bed later that night. They were both wide-awake, the "dinner incident" still fresh in their minds.

"I'll mend it tomorrow, first thing." He turned to his side and stroked her hair. "Libby, I don't care if they're your brothers. They bust in here again like that, I'm gonna hurt somebody."

"But Nate …"

"Darlin'," he interrupted. "They almost hurt you and your sisters."

He had a point, and Libby had to concede. She turned to face him. "I still don't understand what happened. They left so suddenly, before any of us can ask."

"They left because you did ask, remember?"

"Oh, yes …" Libby said, her voice trailing off. After things settled down, and Bonnie started asking their brothers questions, the three lit out of there, refusing to answer. Walt was less than friendly at that moment, and threatened Benedict, Hank, and Percy with dire consequences should they ever set foot on Dalton property again. But where did they go? What will they do now? Hank said something about not being able to go back to Beckham empty-handed. What was that supposed to mean? Just what had been happening back home while Libby and her sisters had been in Texas?

"Libby, my little Libby …" Nate whispered against her hair. "How long have you known?"

"Known?"

"About the baby, sweetheart."

Libby smiled. "I wasn't sure until today."

Nate smiled against her lips, and kissed her. "I think that's the second best Christmas present I've ever gotten."

Libby touched his cheek. "The second? What was the first?"

He kissed her again. "You."

"But I didn't come on Christmas."

"No, you just came early, is all. Merry Christmas, darlin'."

Libby smiled. "Merry Christmas, Nate." She kissed him again, and then gave to him everything she had.

The End

ABOUT THE AUTHOR

A consistent Top 100 bestseller, Kit Morgan, aka Geralyn Beauchamp, has been writing for fun all of her life. When writing as Geralyn Beauchamp, her books are epic, adventurous, romantic fantasy at its best. When writing as Kit Morgan they are whimsical, fun, inspirational sweet stories that depict a strong sense of family and community. Kit's 'His Prairie Princess', is the first of the Prairie Brides books and the first in the series of a long line of stories about Clear Creek, Oregon. One of the wackiest little towns in the old west! Get to know the townsfolk in Clear Creek and come sit a spell! Connect with her at
www.AuthorKitMorgan.com

If you enjoy historical western romances, join us in the **Pioneer Hearts Facebook group**, a place where historical western romance authors and readers discuss their favorite stories, recipes and photos **www.facebook.com/groups/pioneerhearts**

READ THE EXCERPTS AND
LEARN MORE ABOUT THE
RANCHER'S MAIL-ORDER
BRIDE, AND THE DRIFTER'S
MAIL-ORDER BRIDE, AVAILABLE
NOW!

WHAT'S NEXT?

THE RANCHER'S MAIL ORDER BRIDE
BY
KIRSTEN OSBOURNE

Through no fault of her own, Gwen Blue found herself embroiled in a scandal that would set Beckham, Massachusetts on its ear, and get her locked in her room for two months. When she found herself betrothed to a man she found loathsome, she wanted nothing more than to disappear. When her sisters liberated her from her room and proposed a journey to Texas to visit an old school friend, she didn't have to be asked twice.

Walton Dalton always had a plan for his life. He'd spent years learning everything he needed to know about ranching, and he had a large parcel of land adjacent to his two brothers' land. Between the three of them, they were going to build a Texas ranching empire. For his empire, he needed a bride.

Without his brothers' knowledge, Walt sends off for three mail order brides from a matchmaker in Beckham. He knows from the moment he sees 'Gorgeous Gwen' that she's meant to be his. Will she agree to the marriage? If she does, will she be able to get over her self-centered attitude and be a good wife?

EXCERPT

Gwen rushed off the train and immediately started looking around for the stagecoach. Bonnie caught up to her, putting her hand on her sister's shoulder. "Don't run off now!"

"I'm looking for the stagecoach. It's only another three hours, and we'll be there. I can't wait to see Anna." Really, it wasn't so much seeing Anna that she cared about. She needed to be in one place for a while. The journey had been much too long for her.

"You didn't even like Anna," Bonnie argued.

"Well, I love her today, because she's going to let me sleep in a bed that doesn't move!" Gwen looked at Bonnie. "The bed won't move will it? She doesn't live on a boat or something silly like that?"

Bonnie laughed. "No, I don't think the bed will move." She led the way to the platform. "We need to wait for our trunk to be unloaded."

Gwen laughed. "I was so excited to be on the stagecoach, I forgot all about my trunk. That was silly of me, wasn't it?"

Libby and Bonnie exchanged looks. "Our trunk, Gwenny. We could only pack one trunk for the three of us or Mama and Papa would have gotten suspicious."

"Are you serious? You'd better have packed my cornflower blue dress. It's my favorite." Gwen looked between her sisters.

Bonnie sighed. "We couldn't. We didn't have access to your clothes at all, because you were locked in your room, remember? We brought some of Libby's dresses for you."

Gwen made a face. "Libby's dresses? But Libby and I don't look good in the same colors. I'm blond, and Libby's a brunette." Besides, she wanted her own clothes. Clothes that had been made just for her.

"I'll make you a new cornflower blue dress, Gwen. I promise. Just...don't make a fuss."

Gwen looked at her sister, surprised by her words. "A fuss? Why would I make a fuss?" She could see by Bonnie's face something was still wrong. "What were you going to tell me?"

Bonnie sighed. "Well, we're not exactly here to see Anna."

Gwen raised an eyebrow, more than a little annoyed her sisters had lied to her. "Why are we here then?"

"I..." Bonnie avoided Gwen's gaze, something she'd never done.

It must be bad, Gwen thought. If Bonnie can't tell me what's going on, she's done something terrible.

At that moment two men, who were obviously twin brothers, stepped between them. "Are you ladies the Blue sisters?" one of them asked. He had brown eyes and black hair. His shoulders were the broadest she'd ever seen. She wouldn't mind stepping out with him at all.

Gwen nodded slowly. "Who are you?" She'd never seen these men in her life. Why were they looking for them? Were they there to drive them to their new home, wherever it may be? She still didn't know why they were in Texas.

The man who'd asked the question grinned. "I'm Walton Dalton, and I pick you." He grabbed her hand and pulled her into his arms before she had a chance to reply. His mouth covered hers and he kissed her, right there in the middle of the train station.

Gwen stomped on his foot, enjoying the kiss, but she knew it wasn't proper to kiss a man she'd just met. "Unhand me!" She wiped her hand across her mouth, trying to stop the tingling that had started as soon as his lips had met hers.

Walt smiled down at Gwen. "I'll unhand you for now. Preacher's standing by." He kept his arm firmly around his little fiancé's shoulders. "Which sister are you?"

"I'm Gwendolyn. Why do you persist in touching me? I don't know you!" She struggled against him, but realized it was futile. He was much stronger than she would ever be.

Bonnie smiled at Walt. "I'm Bonnie. I'm the oldest sister. I believe I'm the one you're supposed to marry."

Walt looked back and forth between the sisters. "I don't care who's oldest. I'm marrying this one." He nodded at Nate. "That's my brother Nate. Bart should be here by now, but I'm sure he'll be along." He'd better be along. He'd promised Walt he'd be there by three. It was quarter after.

Bonnie glared at Walt and turned to Nate, who was openly staring at Libby. "Libby's the youngest," she announced, seeming to think that would matter to the brothers.

Nate looked back and forth between Walt and Bonnie. "I thought we were here to see a man about some cattle."

Walt grinned at his brother. "Surprise! Since Bart isn't here, you get next pick. Which one do you want for your bride?" He didn't expect a lot of problems from Nate. Bart was the one who would protest the loudest.

Nate blinked. "You sent off for brides for us? The cattle salesman was a lie?"

Walt shrugged. "I didn't think you'd come if I told you why we were really here." He kissed the top of Gwen's head as if they'd been in love for years. "Pick one." He wasn't letting this little beauty go. He'd expected all three sisters to be homely. Gwen had been a fabulous surprise.

Nate pointed at Libby. "I guess I'll take the youngest." He leaned close to Walt and whispered, "I'll take care of you later."

Gwen gasped in shock. "You can't just pick me and say you'll marry me. No! What on earth is happening here. Bonnie? What have you done?" As grateful as Gwen was to her sister for rescuing her, she was furious about this arrangement. She had no desire to marry a stranger or anyone else for that matter.

Bonnie blinked as if fighting tears. "Libby knew why we were here. We just didn't want you to be stubborn. We rescued you after all."

THE DRIFTER'S MAIL ORDER BRIDE
BY
CASSIE HAYES

Having grown up in the shadow of two beautiful sisters, 'Scrawny Bonnie' Blue knows she doesn't stand a chance at landing a good man in Beckham, Massachusetts. The only way she'll find a husband is by leaving her family behind to become a mail order bride. But when all three Blue sisters are swept up in a scandal, she has no choice to but to take 'Gorgeous Gwen' and 'Lovely Libby' with her…kicking and screaming, if she must.

Bart Dalton would be happy riding the range forever, but his brothers need his help to start a ranch in north Texas. He figures he'll last a year or so before his feet get itchy again, which his brothers understand. As triplets, they can almost read each others' minds. Except when his oldest brother orders three brides for them all. It would have been nice to have a little warning about *that!*

When Bart is late to meet the train carrying the Blue sisters, his brothers get first dibs, leaving Bonnie standing alone and dejected once again. It only gets worse when her 'intended' finally shows up and balks at the idea of marrying her. The only thing Bonnie has going for her are her wits, and she puts them to good use by proposing a business arrangement that Bart can't refuse.

Will Bart go back to his drifter ways, or is the elusive thing he's been searching for all his life sleeping in the next room?

EXCERPT

The moment Bonnie and her sisters stepped off the train, she spotted two men who looked identical. The odds of there being a set of twins *and* a set of triplets meeting that particular train seemed low, so she assumed the third brother was simply out of sight.

Raising a tentative hand to the men, she started across the platform with Libby and a clueless Gwen, who was prattling on about the stagecoach ride they were supposed to be taking into Wiggieville to see Anne. The men met them halfway.

"Are you ladies the Blue sisters?" asked one of the men.

"Who are you?" Gwen said, as rude as ever.

"I'm Walton Dalton, and I pick you," replied the man. Then he did the most amazing thing. He pulled Gwen into a kiss — right there on the platform in front of God and everyone!

Gwen took care of him, though, by stomping on his foot, but he didn't seem deterred. In fact, he seemed more determined than ever, going so far as to say the preacher was standing by. And poor Gwen had no idea what was going on.

"Mr. Dalton," Bonnie said, addressing Walton and trying to keep the panic from her voice, "I'm Bonnie. I'm the oldest sister." He seemed completely nonplussed by this news so she elaborated further. "I believe I'm the one you're supposed to marry."

"I don't care who's oldest," he said, gazing down at Gwen. "I'm marrying this one."

He might just as well have punched Bonnie in the stomach. She'd come all this way expecting to marry the eldest brother and who had he gone for? Gwen, of course. She shouldn't have been surprised, really, but it still stung.

"I believe your letter said there would be three of you," she managed to squeak out.

"That's my brother Nate," Walton said, nodding at his brother before flicking his eyes around the platform. "Bart should be here by now but I'm sure he'll be along."

Bonnie didn't really care about the inconsiderate brother Bart, who couldn't be bothered to keep an appointment. She had higher expectations from her future husband.

She turned to look at Nate but he couldn't seem to rip his gaze away from Libby, who was blushing furiously and peeking up at him from behind her dark lashes. This wouldn't do at all. She refused to be the consolation prize for the one who didn't show up on time.

"Libby's the youngest!" she fairly shouted, drawing surprised looks from everyone. Surely he would do the right thing and choose Bonnie over her baby sister. But of course Nate had been just as surprised as Gwen at the situation he'd found himself in and he simply looked confused.

To his credit, he adapted much more quickly than Gwen did, as soon as Walton explained, but Bonnie once again found herself ignored and rejected in favor of her prettier sisters. Bitterness settled over her heart at the realization her life would be no different outside of Beckham.

And now...now she was leftovers. The discarded garbage the other two brothers didn't want. She was table scraps! It was all she could do to choke back the tears as they waited for the tardy youngest brother.

What had she been thinking, bringing her sisters along? She'd registered with Elizabeth's mail order bride agency to leave Beckham — including her family — behind. With nothing to compare her to, her future husband might have been pleased with her. She was extremely skilled at homemaking and, when not standing next to her beautiful sisters, she wasn't altogether homely.

She'd ruined her entire life by putting the welfare of her sisters ahead of her own, just as she'd always done. Never once growing up had they shown her the same courtesy, so why did she feel so responsible for them? They certainly didn't refuse the advances of Walt and Nate, even though Bonnie made it very clear she expected to be the first chosen.

For five full minutes, she sat on that bench and hated her sisters. She wished and prayed for a runaway train to jump the tracks and barrel across the platform, taking them all with it. She would be the lone survivor, and the only person to turn up at the group funeral. Of course, she would be draped in black but behind her dark veil, she would be smiling. Maybe even laughing.

Then Libby reached over and squeezed her hand. The poor child was trembling. Bonnie's frozen heart melted, and she gave her youngest sister an encouraging smile. She couldn't begrudge either sister happiness, nor would she wish misery on them. And marrying those lecherous old deacons would have been a life sentence of misery.

Well, if she couldn't have love, she would at least do everything in her power to make sure her sisters were happy and cared for. If these two men, who were so entranced by their beauty, didn't do right by them, they'd have Bonnie to answer to.

As for her, she had little choice but to accept the errant Dalton as her husband. What little money they had left after the train journey wouldn't be enough for her to buy a meal, much less a ticket back home. The question was, would he accept her?

It looked like she was about to find out. Walton was striding across the platform to meet with a third man who looked just like him. As late as Bart was meeting them, Bonnie would have thought he'd have a little giddy-up in his get-along, but in fact he seemed quite unperturbed. Clearly the man was unreliable, inconsiderate and untrustworthy.

Wonderful.

Bonnie was just thinking that maybe marrying Deacon Smith would have been preferable to a layabout ne'er-do-well when Walt led his brother over to make introductions. Swallowing her pride — what was left of it, anyway — she stood and did her best to not glare at the man. Alienating him before he even found out they were to be married wouldn't help matters.

But the moment Bart's deeply tanned and calloused hand enveloped hers, the second his rich brown eyes met her own, all the words — every word she'd ever learned — flew right out of her head. A strange drumming roared in her ears, and she was surprised to discover it was her heart beating wildly. The palm he was holding so gently in his strong hand was suddenly wet with perspiration. Bonnie had never been left speechless in her life, and she didn't understand her strange reaction to this man.

But the spell was broken when Walt introduced her as Bart's bride. The look of sheer horror that flashed across his face was enough to bring her out of her stupor. Her brain was still trying to play catch-up but two words managed to rise to the surface. Two words that would show she was no one to be trifled with. Two words that would perfectly signify her disdain for him.

"You're late."

Manufactured by Amazon.ca
Bolton, ON

35740391R00111